Andrew

Every Day Papers

Vol. 1

SALZWASSER
VERLAG

Andrew Halliday

Every Day Papers

Vol. 1

Reprint of the original, first published in 1864.

1st Edition 2022 | ISBN: 978-3-75259-370-9

Verlag (Publisher): Salzwasser Verlag GmbH, Zeilweg 44, 60439 Frankfurt, Deutschland
Vertretungsberechtigt (Authorized to represent): E. Roepke, Zeilweg 44, 60439 Frankfurt, Deutschland
Druck (Print): Books on Demand GmbH, In de Tarpen 42, 22848 Norderstedt, Deutschland

EVERY DAY PAPERS.

VOL. I.

EVERY DAY PAPERS.

BY

ANDREW HALLIDAY.

IN TWO VOLUMES.

VOL. I.

LONDON

1864.

PREFACE.

The following papers have already appeared in *All the Year Round* and other publications.* The favour with which some of them were received and noticed by the press at the time of their first appearance induces me to offer them to the public in a collected form. Some of the papers are no doubt trivial enough, but I am proud to believe—indeed, to know—that a few of them, particularly "My Account with Her Majesty" and "Exceedingly Odd Fellows," have done considerable good, by calling attention to the advantages of the Post-office Savings Banks, and the disadvantages of ill-managed Benefit Societies. "My Account with Her Majesty"

* *The Train*, *London Society*, *National Magazine*, &c.

has been published, by permission of Mr Charles Dickens, as a penny tract, and also in the *British Workman*: by which means, I am assured, it has reached the hands of nearly half a million of working men. This paper has also had the honour of being printed in slips and distributed among the Post-office Savings Banks throughout the country, for the information and encouragement of depositors.

In respect of these papers, and some others of a similar kind, I am in hopes that my volumes may serve to "combine instruction with amusement."

ANDREW HALLIDAY.

London, Oct. 20th, 1864.

CONTENTS OF VOL. I.

EVERY DAY PAPERS.

TRAGIC CASE OF A COMIC WRITER.

The poet is born, not made. I am made, not born. All the world of editors and managers of theatres has conspired to make me a comic writer, when nature intended me for a serious one. I was made to write poems in blank verse and in cantos; editors have made me write crambo rhymes to fill up half-pages. Nature designed that I should lucubrate for the high-heeled sock; managers have resolved that I shall scribble for the low-heeled buskin. Do what I will, I cannot escape from the thrall of these tyrants, who who have leagued themselves together to pervert my genius to base uses. If I propose to a publisher to write him a three-volume novel, he smiles at me incredulously, and says: "Not in your line; can't you give me a bundle of those light, comic, trifles which you know so well how to hit off?" Hit off, indeed! I hate hitting off. I never hit off. I ponder, I excogitate, I burn the midnight oil, I study; and this dull, unperceptive fellow asks me to "hit off" something. I should like to hit him off. I assure the reader, on my honour as a gentleman, and, let me add, a scholar, that my blank verse is of a very high order indeed. Friends have said "equal to Tennyson," and I am not disposed to accuse them of flattery. But what happens to my blank verse? Invariably and consistently "declined with thanks." Professing and practising various branches of the literary art, as is the custom, now-a-days, I contribute to the leading columns of the newspapers: my forte is politics. All, who have the pleasure of my acquaintance in the private circle, know that I could come out strong in party strife; but where is the editor who will allow me to write a political leader? Echo answers, where? When I go down to the office in the afternoon, fully expecting to be put on to Church-rates or Schleswig-Holstein, what do I find? Why, that Church-rates and Schleswig-Holstein have been served out to two of the greatest idiots in the universe; and I—I, forsooth, who could shake the whole bench of bishops in their square-toed shoes and crumple up Germany with half a quire of note-paper—*I* am obliged to be content with the smallest crumbs that fall from the editorial table. "Crasher, you had better write about that police case—make it light and readable; or you may take up the nurse-maid and perambulator question—smart, you know, smart."

The first of the month comes round, and there is reviewing to be done. I hasten to the office, in the hope of being entrusted with a history in fourteen volumes, or somebody's political life and times. Do I get them? Of course not. They are carried off by the two dullest bores in the universe, and the impenetrable editor hands me the monthly parts of the penny periodicals, concerning which I am expected to say that they sustain their reputation, and are fully up to their usual standard—which, I take this unfettered opportunity of declaring, is very low indeed. Why don't I remonstrate? I do. And what do I get by it? "Stick to your line, my good sir, and that is the light, the airy, the amusing." The light! the airy! the amusing! I, who have read Thucydides in the original, and waded to the last chapter of Alison!

I have the distinguished honour, also, to write for the monthly magazines. There is nothing of which I am more firmly convinced than that I am the man to write a sensation story to run through twenty numbers, and be published afterwards in three volumes, with a portrait of the author. But catch any editor letting me. *I* should like to catch one at it very much. "No, my dear sir; Spindler does those things—it's his line; yours, you know, is the touch-and-go sort of thing. Let me have one of your light sketches, something like 'Up a Tree,' or 'Down a Well,' or 'Over the Bender'—something sharp and *short*. Mind, not above five pages, for Spindler's story is long this month." Yes—confound him; it always is long—and dreary. I never could, never shall, understand why Spindler is allowed to spin out so many pages of that dull trash every month. Everybody yawns over it. Nobody likes it. The editor doesn't like it. Still, he maintains the opinion that Spindler is the man for the continued story. It is acknowledged that I am smart, readable, entertaining; yet Spindler is permitted to huddle me up into a corner. If Spindler takes a fancy to spin out, I must cut down. I must wait upon Spindler—fill in his hollow places. Pad him, in fact. And, between you and me, reader, I know Spindler to be an ass.

Then, again, there is my friend and patron, the manager of the Theatre Royal. Ask him what he thinks of Crasher? "Clever fellow, smart fellow; devilish smart, and no mistake!" But let me propose a comedy or a drama to him. What then? Why he turns the subject, and asks me if I have thought about the Christmas burlesque? or if I could not do a little *pièce de circonstance* for him? "Hit off something of the day," he says; "the Exhibition; the Japanese Ambassadors—something that will play half an hour, and make the people roar." There it is again; I must always be hitting off something. And I must make the audience roar with laughter when I want to make them weep. Now I know that it is much more difficult to make people laugh than to make them cry; but then you don't get so much kudos for laughter as for tears. A bit of claptrap sentiment is "fine feeling," "exquisite pathos," and so forth, in the review; a side-splitting witticism, or a stroke of humour, is simply "an amusing absurdity."

Besides, a little grief goes a great way. Melt your audience to tears twice in the course of three long acts, and your drama is a success. But in a farce, or a burlesque, you must produce incessant laughter, or you are voted dull. You must shake the walls; you must make the pit sway to and fro in convulsions; you must cause the genteel people in the boxes to roll themselves ungenteely on the red velvet cushions; you must cause ribs to ache, and the eyes overflow. In three acts you may venture to be respectable; but in a farce—a mere trifle, an absurdity—nothing short of the great convulsion of human nature—that of making people laugh till they cry—will satisfy the public, and, let me add, the manager. I have found out what the manager of the Royal Screamer does on the first nights of my farces. For some time I flattered myself that he sat in a private box to enjoy my productions in common with the public. I have been cruelly undeceived. He sits up-stairs in his room, writing his letters —leaving the door open to hear whether the people laugh or not. If his critical ear should catch a prolonged roar every other second, he is satisfied that the piece is a good one, and pays without a murmur. But if there be anything like wide gaps of time between the roars—say a minute and a half—he will probably propose a reduction.

Now look at the cruelty and injustice of this proceeding! Suppose I were employed to write five-act comedies—for which high class of drama I am peculiarly fitted—would the manager then be able to judge of my productions from distant echoes? Certainly not. The test of a comedy is not laughter. A comedy does not require to be funny. Speaking of modern comedy, I am confirmed in the opinion that the one essential requisite of pieces of that class is a negative one. If they don't make the people absolutely hiss, they are a success, and their authors are dignified with the name of dramatists; while I, whose merits are of the most positive kind, am set down as a writer of "trifles."

How do the critics notice Shakespeare Smith's comedy in five acts? Well, they don't say it is good—how should they? But they devote a column to it, and exalt it with the name of a "work;" while I am disposed of in a few hasty lines, though it is admitted that I sent the audience home with aching sides. Shakespeare Smith, who, I have no hesitation in saying, is imbecile, gets credit for "works." I—born a true poet—am dubbed a farceur. The taunt pursues me even to the domestic circle and the social board. Does not my friend M'Fling open upon me at our club suppers in the terrible accents of Clackmannan, and ask, in the intervals of shouting for mair toddy, why I don't write "worrks?" "Write worrks, sir," roars M'Fling; "worrrks, worrrrks"—and he snaps his fingers at me in contempt. Why, I ask, is Shakespeare Smith, who is known by every one of his acquaintance to be a dull dog—with some slight knowledge of the French language—why is this person to be exalted above me? Because of his superior talent? No; simply because he writes in five dull acts, instead of in one single lively act. He writes worrks.

And there is the sensation dramatist: that great man of this age of thunder, whose treasury is a golden mint, who resides in a palatial mansion and drives down to the dingy stage-door in a magnificent chariot. If you were to get at this illustrious man's opinion of himself (and it is not difficult to obtain), you would probably find that he places himself on the same pedestal with Shakespeare—I don't mean Shakespeare Smith, but Shakespeare of Avon. Now here am I occupying a Bloomsbury first floor and riding down to the Screamer on rehearsal days—only on wet ones—in the twopenny 'bus. Why is this? Do you mean to tell me that I could not write sensation dramas and coin my own money, if I had the chance? Could not I buy a shilling book at a stall—or, in default of the shilling, borrow one—and make a drama out of it? And would it be a work of surperhuman genius in me, or, in the words of the classic orator, any other man, to write in at the end of the second act as a stage direction, "Here the villain carries the heroine off in a balloon; the lover arrives, fires a rifle at the villain, who tumbles to the earth, and the heroine descends in safety in a parachute, extemporized out of her crinoline?" I really must be allowed to say that my genius is equal to this. But where is the manager who will allow me to take so short and easy a road to fame and fortune? I pause for a reply. No response. Of course not. "Stick to your farces and burlesques, my boy. These big works are not in your line; leave them to Pouncer and Bouncer."

Now, look you, my friends, I am well acquainted with Pouncer. I have taken stock of his mental machinery, and know every spring and cog in it. In fact, he has taken the whole machine to pieces, and laid it before me repeatedly. What I say, then, of the case, Pouncer, is, that it encloses a very common movement. No escapement, no jewelled holes, no three-quarter plate—quite a common verge affair. Why do I not stand in the shoes—patent leather —of Pouncer? Be it understood I envy no man; but quite in an abstract way, and as a question of art, I repeat, Why do I not stand in the high-heeled patent leathers of Pouncer? Simply for this reason:—Pouncer and I went out one day without shoes, and it happened quite by accident that Pouncer stumbled upon that high-heeled patent leather pair, while I, less favoured by fate, or fortune, fell in with these low-heeled slippers. Perhaps you ask why, if I am so much stronger than Pouncer, I did not hustle him, and take the patent leathers from him? Not so easy a matter as you imagine. When the world catches you in a good pair of shoes it nails them to your feet; or, with the same even-handed injustice, let it catch you in down-at-heel slippers, and it nails, it clenches, them upon you. I am firmly persuaded that if I had had the good fortune to stumble upon the shoes, Pouncer would have worn out the slippers in treading the walks of Profound Obscurity.

One, with whom I have everything in common, has said, "All the world's a stage." Let me carry out the simile in a certain way, and add, perforated with round and square holes—and all the men and women merely pegs. Now I am thoroughly convinced that, with a few exceptions, a perverse fate fills all the round holes with square pegs, and vice versâ. I am a square peg, and I fill a round hole; fill it well, certainly, and don't wabble about as some square pegs would do in the situation; but why am I not in the rectangular orifice designed for me? I know why. Happening to slip in here to see how I should fit, I was stamped into the place before I could get out again. All my enemies, the moment they caught me in the hole, came in a troop and hammered away at me, one after the other, until now my fine edges are worn off, and I am hopelessly jammed in.

I see about me a great many pegs, round and square, all filling the wrong holes in a most inadequate manner. The majority of them, however, have reason to rejoice that they find themselves in any hole whatever. There is the peg Spindler. It is popularly supposed that he fits his hole neatly. I tell you he has been plugged in there. Take him up, pull him out—like a paving-stone or a brick—and throw him among a heap of his fellows. He may pass muster in a job-lot; but when the paviour or the mason comes to single him out, he will not be thought worth the re-dressing.

Then there are my friends, the two idiots. Why are they selected for the heavy business? Because the solemnity of their dulness was mistaken in early life for profundity. Because they were never seen to smile; because they were never known to make a joke; because they are ugly; because they have big heads; because they are old; because Time has rusted them in their holes. Pouncer, again. How is it that he fills so important a place? Because, without any special fitness for any hole whatever, he has always been a candidate for every hole vacant. Fortune is fickle; but a pertinacious man may bother her out of her life. Pouncer has bothered her out of her life.

The greatest authority on Russian affairs of the present time, is a man who once paid a visit of ten days to his aunt at Riga. He learned all about the serf question during those ten days at Riga. If a history of Russia were wanted, Jobbins would be sent for to do it. Why has Hornby acquired a reputation for the possession of profound scientific knowledge? Because, early in life, he wore the hair off the top of his head, mounted spectacles, dressed at all times in a swallow-tailed black coat, and constantly let people catch him perusing a scientific treatise. It was a good-dodge of Hornby to turn his bald head and weak eyes to scientific account. It pays.

Viewing on all hands this ill-assorted array of pegs, I have come to a very grand and comprehensive conclusion. It is this: that the few cases throughout history in which the right man has been in the right place, have been the results of accident. Accident, which has put so many men in the wrong place, has put a few—a very few—in the right. Shakespeare found the right hole; so did Milton; so did Hampden; so did Newton; so did Watt; so did some others that are thinly dotted over the stage of time. In these latter days, however, there are more pins, and the stage has not extended its dimensions. We are crowded; we hustle each other; and in the scrimmage the wrong men drop into the holes, and, in the hurry and bustle of our life, are trodden into them until they seem to fit. I firmly believe that there are village Hampdens and mute inglorious Miltons in scores among us. All they want is an accident to slip them into the right holes. I am not sure whether I am a village Hampden, or a mute inglorious Milton; but I am satisfied I should have been somebody very big indeed, if I had not begun my career by writing that popular work—the "Romance of a Kidney Pudding." How solidly famous I might have been by this time had I started with a treatise on the Cosmogony, or something of that sort!

I hear a whole chorus of voices openly rebuking me. Do I not have my reward? Do I not get more for one of my trashy pieces than was paid to Goldsmith for his glorious Vicar, or to Milton for his immortal Paradise Lost? Are not my trumpery farces announced in the papers long before their production; are they not criticised next day in all the journals, as if they were works of the highest importance? There is my name blazing amid the record of imperial affairs.

The eye of the reader cannons off Lord Palmerston on to the Pope, off the Pope on to Garibaldi, off Garibaldi on to Crasher, and there it rests in admiration.

Disappointed, rejected, and oppressed aspirants of high art tendencies, do not, I pray, heap coals of fire upon my head! Think you that I take pride in being glorified as a suckler of fools and a chronicler of small beer? Besides, I would ask you if this is more than my reward? What, do you imagine are the feelings of a man with a soul like mine, who, in the course of a work, has to crush a new hat, cause a fellow-creature to be knocked into a bandbox, and smash a whole trayful of cups and saucers? Is there to be no compensation for injured feelings and outraged nature? At the same time I am willing to admit that you, my ten-canto poet—you, my grave and learned essayist—you, my high art dramatist, should be glorified in that column, not I. Go, persuade them to admit your claim to that consideration which you deserve, and I will stand aside. I am willing to contend with you for the high-heeled shoes, when the judge awards them to him who fills them best.

PANTALOON.

I AM a pantaloon, lean and slippered, and fast sinking into that last stage when, as Shakespeare says, I shall be sans eyes, sans teeth, sans taste, sans everything. At present, thank Heaven, I can see pretty well with my specs, and as to teeth and taste, I have more of both than is quite convenient. I have a mighty fine taste for a roast duck, but it's seldom that such a delicacy comes my way. Seldom, did I say? Never. I haven't tasted roast duck these seven year, not since Joey took this public-house. Joey gave a jollification on that occasion, and well he might, to me at least. I played pantaloon to Joey's clown, off and on, for nigh five-and-thirty years, and he had a heavy hand—a heavy foot too. He was always very rough at his business. If I missed the slap, Joey would give me a real one, a regular stinger; and the people in the front liked the real thing best. They always laughed more at the real thing, and that encouraged Joey to do the real thing. Once, when he nearly broke my back with the barber's shutter, the gallery went into regular convulsions, and shouted "Encore." Joey was for doing it again; but I wouldn't have it. This half murder style of thing was what Joey called holding the mirror up to nature; but I didn't see it. I've had an awful life with Joey, and that's the truth. He has kicked and cuffed and battered me into what I am—a shaky old pantaloon, stiff at the joints, and weak about the small of the back—scarcely worth my salt, even outside a booth. But Joey—Joey keeps this first-class public that we're now in, and Joey drives his own gig, and wears a big diamond ring on his finger, and carries a gold watch that cost forty guineas, with a large gold chain that spreads out all over his beautiful crimson-velvet waistcoat, and makes him look like a Duke. Yes, like a Duke. On Sundays, when he drives down the Edgeware-road in his gig, Joey looks like the Duke I saw go up in the balloon along with Mrs Graham.

Joey has been a lucky dog all through. He married a lady—a real lady, and no mistake—far superior to Joey. She's one of those delicate creatures that lies a-bed half the day; but when she *does* get up, she can speak French and play the piano, like a good 'un. She don't often come into the bar until evening, when the gas is lighted; and then she looks like the last scene in a pantomime. She's a regular walking blaze of triumph, with diamonds—real ones. Ah! It makes me think when I'm a-sitting here in this jug and bottle department, smoking my pipe and seeing them glittering fingers of hers drawing me half a pint of the best porter! "Lor' bless me," I says to myself, "what a thing is Fortun!" Joey and me started together. I had the best headpiece of the two; that was allowed. I had a bit of schooling—Joey had never a morsel. I could do the high trap leap cleaner than Joey. I wasn't quite so good at the hornpipe, but I could dance it, and play the tune on the fiddle at the same time; and Joey, he couldn't play a bit. But look at us now! Joey is down at Hornsey-wood House, pigeon-shooting, togged out to the nines, drinking champagne with the swells, and flashing his diamonds and his gold chains with the best of them; while here am I, a sitting on this here barrel, enjoying the only luxury I can afford—half a pint of porter and a pipe, with the privilege of being allowed to chat with Madame Pollonio.

Here she comes, now that the gas is turned on. Look at her rings! Don't they glitter beautiful when she takes hold of the ivory handle of the beer engine, and passes them backwards and forwards under the lights! Pollonio ain't Joey's right name, of course; he took it just as I took the name of Devanti. There was a rage for foreigners when we were in the country together, some five-and-twenty years ago. A lot of sprites and contortionists come over and called themselves Signor this and Herr that; and they were all the go. At that time Joey and I were engaged to go to London, to the Bower, to play in the pantomime at Christmas, and I says to Joey,

"Let's be foreigners, Joey, and change our names; I'll be a Signor and you be a Herr."

"No, no, hang it," says Joey; "I'll be the Signor, and you be the Herr."

"Very well," I says, "I don't mind"—Joey always had the best of it—"you be the Signor if you like. Now what shall we change our names to?"

"Oh," says Joey—he always had an eye to the main chance—"let it be something like our own names, in case anybody should leave us a legacy."

"Good," says I, though I wasn't much afraid of that myself. After a long consultation and much twisting and turning about of our names, it was settled between us that "Joe Pollard" should be transformed into "Signor Pollonio," and "Alfred Davis" into "Herr Devanti."

This was the turning-point in our fortuns; at least not my fortuns, but Joey's. Mine were all misfortuns, and no fault of my own neither. You know what my opinion of Joey is. He ain't a bad fellow; but he has no headpiece, and he can't play the fiddle and dance the hornpipe at the same time. I'm not a bit conceited; but I always was a better man than Joey, and I am sure as I'm born, that if it hadn't been for the unlucky turn up of a halfpenny, I shouldn't be a sitting here now on this barrel, drinking of humble porter. I should be down at Hornsey-wood House pigeon-shooting, and drinking champagne with swells—that's where I should be. I can see that fatal halfpenny now. It was a Friday—always an unlucky day with me—and it was the last remaining coin of my week's salary, which, being then at Barnsley, I needn't tell you, wasn't heavy to carry home. I had been turning the halfpenny over and looking at it all the afternoon, for there was nothing that I could spend it in, but apples or sweetstuff, and I did not care about them. It was an old George the Third halfpenny, worn as smooth as a button on the Woman's side, and with nothing left for the King's head on the other, but a little round bulge in the copper, like a sun blister on a brown door. I should know that halfpenny again, among a thousand. I have reason.

After the performances that night, Joey and I got talking about our London engagement. We were to go up in the second week in December to arrange the comic business and rehearse. Now, I was very anxious about one point. It was an arrangement between Joey and me in the country that we should play clown, time about. When Joey played it at one town, it was my turn to play it at the next town; and then Joey played pantaloon. At Barnsley Joey was playing clown. The next place would be London; so I says to Joey,

"It's my turn to play clown next."

Joey had his head in the basin then, washing off the paint, and he didn't answer. I repeated the words, "It's my turn to play clown next time, Joey." I never knew Joey take such a long time to wash off the paint before. He kept on slousing and puffing and spluttering, just like a porpoise, and I thought he *would* never have done. At last he took his head out of the basin, and began drying himself.

"You heard what I said, Joey?"

"Of course I did," Joey says; "your turn next, that's right; and look here, Alf, old boy, you shall have it to-morrow. We'll see Grundler before we go, and get him to alter the names in the bill, and you shall play clown for the rest of the engagement."

Artful Joey! This was the scheme he was

making up under the water in the basin. If I took clown now, it would be his turn when we went to London.

"No, no, Joey," I says, "none of that; I'm in no hurry; I can wait till we go to London, Joey."

Joey saw that I was up to his scheme, and turned rusty. We had a long altercation over it, and at last Joey began to brag of his superior qualifications for the part. He was younger, he said, and was better at the hornpipe. "Allowed," said I; "but you can't play the fiddle with it; and I'm told the double business is a great go in London." He could do the stilts; but I could walk the barrel. He could turn a double somersault; I was good at Tippetywitchet and Hot Codlins. We come to high words, and were nigh breaking up the partnership, but Joey suddenly calmed down, and said:

"Alf, we've been friends now some years; don't let us quarrel; come away and have a drain." So we went into the Nag's Head, and Joey stood rum-and-water, which was put down to him. We had two stiff glasses, and then walked away towards home together. Joey never said a word for some time, nor I neither; but suddenly, when I was coming close to my lodging, he stopped and held out his hand to me; and I took it.

"Don't let us quarrel, Alf," he says; "this is a new start altogether; let's toss for it, that's the fairest way." And he grasped my hand kindly. I couldn't help being touched by Joey's friendly way.

"Agreed," says I; "it is, as you say, a new start, and tossing is as fair for the one as it is for the other."

Joey felt in his pocket for a coin, but he was at a lower ebb than me. He hadn't got e'er a one. I produced my halfpenny.

"What do you say, Joey, will you cry to me?"

"All right," he says; and we drew close to a little chandler's shop where a tallow dip was a glimmering among some herrings and nuts and other odds and ends in the window.

"Which shall it be, Joey, two out of three, or sudden death?"

"Sudden death," says Joey, rather excited, "and I call heads!"

I threw up the halfpenny, intending to catch it, but it fell with a ring on the pavement.

"Hands off!" cried Joey; and we both fell upon our knees in the wet to see what it was.

"It's a woman," I cried out, before I saw it; for the wish was father to the thought, and I was excited.

"No, it ain't," said Joey; "it's a man."

And the tallow dip in the window threw just light enough to show me the brown sun blister that I had been looking at all the afternoon. There was no use denying it. It *was* heads.

"And I play clown in London!" says Joey.

We parted, and I went home to my garret with a heavy heart, to think what a fool I had been to trust to chance what I was entitled to claim as a right. I dreamed that Joey and me tossed again, two out of three, and that I won; but the morning brought back the memory of the halfpenny lying head upwards on the stones underneath the chandler's window. Joey was to play clown in London.

We had a spare week after the end of our engagement at Barnsley, and I went to see some relations at Coventry, promising to meet Joey on a certain day at a public-house close by the Bower.

I met him on the evening appointed. He was in the parlour, surrounded by a lot of people, smoking and drinking and listening with all their ears to Joey. I could see, too, that they were feasting their eyes upon him. I wasn't prepared for the change in Joey's appearance. He was togged out in first-rate style, in a shaggy white great-coat with a velvet collar. He had a large ring on his finger too, and studs in his shirt-front, and a watch-guard that looked as good as gold. Joey had bested me again. I had never given my appearance a thought, and though I had my best things on, I looked shabby and mean by the side of Joey. However, he greeted me kindly in the old way, and introduced me to the company by my new name: "Herr Devanti, the Pantaloon," said Joey, with a magnificent wave of the hand, "my friend and fellow artist. He will play pantaloon to me at the Bower." The company made way for me; but I felt it was only because I was a friend of Signor Pollonio's. I could see that Joey was a great gun among them already.

We come out at the Bower and made a hit, but Joey was the favourite; for, you see, the clown always has the best of it, however good the pantaloon may be. I often heard the boys in the street talking about the pantomime. They said,

"Ain't Signor Pollonio a stunning clown!" but they rarely said anything about me. When anybody did say anything about me, it was:

"Devanti is good as pantaloon." And then some one else would answer,

"Yes—he ain't bad."

Joey carried all before him. The clown, don't you see, has the upper hand in the piece. He makes fun of everybody, knocks everybody about, even the police, and never comes to much harm himself. This sort of character, it seems to me, always gets well thought of in the world. It's the way in our profession at any rate, and I dare say it's the same in other things. Well, I shouldn't complain of that if it didn't rob others of their due. But what's the use of talent, when it's only used to be scored off? If Joey Grimaldi himself had tossed up for his line and won pantaloon, I don't believe we should ever have heard of him. It's like skittles. You talk about the man who gets the floorers, but you never think of the pins. And yet the pins are something; if they don't stand upright to be hit, they won't go down. I was in for it from that very night that I played pantaloon at the Bower. I tried hard to get a clown's engagement afterwards, but it was no go. I might just as well have tried for Archbishop of Canterbury. It had gone forth in London—

"Herr Devanti, the Pantaloon." And pantaloon I was doomed to remain.

I soon got reconciled to my fate; but pantalooning is bad for a man's spirits, bad for his manners, bad for his opinion of himself. Clowning is different; clowning brings a man out—makes him hold up his head, and feel himself somebody as he walks the streets. It gives him confidence, or, perhaps, what some might call cheek. Lor', you should have seen how Joey improved after a month of good salary and success at the Bower. He came out a tremendous swell. Such glossy hats, with braid all round them! Such fluffy white great-coats! Such jewelry! All the young women about the neighbourhood were in love with him. I might have dressed out too, and I thought of doing it once, but I soon lost heart. I felt that it wasn't for a pantaloon to be a swell. People didn't seem to care about staring after the pantaloon. And yet I was as well made and as good-looking as Joey. But the pantalooning work takes the pride and spirit out of a man. At least it did out of me, and I think you'll find it will out of you, if you'll try it yourself. Most pantaloons are about the same.

It wasn't long before I found myself carrying my stage life out into the streets with me, so that the folks said they could tell I was pantaloon by my walk. As for Joey, I have known him to be taken for the Marquis of Waterford. You should have seen how he used to swell up and down Bow-street on Saturdays among seedy actors waiting about there for the ghost to walk; and how the poor devils used to look at him and admire him. Lor' bless you, I've known a leading man, out of collar, say "sir" to Joey.

After that unlucky turn up of the halfpenny Joey had the best of me in everything. He was applauded by the public, petted by the hangers-on about the theatre, treated by the swells, and admired by all the women. And I need not tell you that he always got a much larger salary than I did. The clown always gets more money than the pantaloon. A manager scarcely takes the pantaloon into account. If he gets a good clown, that's all he troubles himself about. He trusts to the clown to find his own pantaloon, as he find his own wigs and his own shoes. There was just one thing, only one, in which I rather got the better of Joey, and I'll leave you to judge if I have reason to rejoice over it. Now mind; I don't say a word myself, one way or another.

One season, a good many years ago now, Joey and I both fell in love with the columbine. She was a pretty girl and clever, and as good as she was both. Joey courted her all he knew, and so did I; but spite of fine clothes and diamond rings, she preferred me, and we were married. Poor thing, she has been disabled from dancing for some years past, by the rheumatics; but she is the mother of my children, and she has always worked hard when she could, and she is a good soul as ever lived. Joey didn't speak to me for a year after I married her, till one night he came into my dressing-room—I dressed with the supers—and showed me a pink three-cornered note that a lady had sent round to him from the boxes. It was an invitation to go and see her at her own house. I heard nothing more of this for a month, when Joey come in again one night, and said:

"Alf, old boy, I'm going to be married."

"Who to?" says I.

Says he, "The lady as sent the letter round from the boxes. She *will* have me; and she's good-looking, Alf; skin likealabaster" (alablaster Joey always called it, for he was no scholar and ain't now), "and she has plenty of money and keeps her carriage."

It was true what Joey said. There's the very lady across the bar there, with the diamond rings a glittering on her fingers. Joey married her—or rather she married Joey—and Joey went the pace with her money, but drew up just in time to settle down in this snug public-house, doing the best over-the-counter trade in the neighbourhood. Joey will be home presently to supper. I hear the missus (Madame Pollonio they call her) tell the girl to put the pheasant down to the fire, a quarter of an hour ago.

Oh yes; Joey askes me to supper sometimes, he's good for that; but he won't to-night. He'll be tired with his day's pigeon-shooting with the swells. Never mind, I have a bit of cheese and an onion in the cupboard at home. That's not a grand supper, I know, but then my business ain't like Joey's. Sweetstuff and toys ain't so profitable as they were. The children have farthing's-worths now-a-days. It's nearly all farthing's-worths, and it's very aggravating when you've got up a ladder, at the risk of your neck, to take down a farthing kite from the top shelf, to see the kid change its mind and run out of the shop to buy apples at the other shop over the way. Well! The bread and cheese might have been pheasant if that unlucky halfpenny had turned up a woman. *Might*, did I say? Must! I tell you, I am certain of it.

SNOBSON'S EXPERIENCES.

I AM thankful to say that I have not hitherto seen many of the downs of life; but, if Fortune has been kind to me in this respect, I am bound to admit that she has not gone to any violent extreme in treating me to a sight of the ups. I have never yet got the length of a carriage—even in the shape of a miniature brougham; and I don't mind confessing that I never had belonging to me, at any one period of my life, a clear sum of a hundred pounds. I once had sixty, free of the world, and it nearly turned my brain. The possession of those sixty pounds, all in sovereigns, made me restless and excited for a whole day and a whole night. I could not work, I could not sleep, for four-and-twenty hours. They even took away my appetite. But, being a bit of a philosopher, and not avaricious, I said to myself:

"Snobson, if the possession of sixty pounds has this effect upon you, what would be your conduct if you were suddenly to become the possessor of sixty thousand? Multiplying that loud tone and that stiffness of back with which the smaller sum afflicts you, in the same ratio, what would be the result in personal assertion, extravagance, and snobbishness?" I did not work out the problem, because I was rather afraid of the solution. I preferred taking warning from several miserable cases in point.

Fortune has terribly thinned in a few years my old circle of friends and acquaintances. Some she has placed beyond my reach by lifting them up—for few of us can bear, with an equal mind, an excess of sovereigns; others she has estranged from me by letting them down. A round dozen of good fellows, whom I can conjure up in my mind's eye sitting at a table on terms of the closest friendship and the warmest fellowship, have parted company, and all for the matter of a few sovereigns more or less.

There is poor Shuffleton. When I first knew him he kept his carriage—two or three carriages for that matter—and I don't know how many horses. He had a fine house in Belgravia. He dressed most expensively, and never wore a coat for more than a month. I never knew him to drink beer. He smoked the choicest cigars, and never condescended to use coppers. He always put his coppers in the pocket of his carriage, and the tiger swept them out every night as he swept out the mud and the dust. Ah, what a fine gentleman Shuffleton was! I admired him much, for he was in all respects a gentleman. He did not cast off his coats at the end of the month and despise coppers from ostentation, but because he was really a rich man. But Shuffleton came to sad grief. He embarked his fortune in an enterprise which turned out a complete failure. He did not lose quite all, but it was a mere wreck that was left to him; and, when this was gone, Shuffleton sank lower and lower, until he reached the very bottom of the pit of poverty. I have seen him in a shabby coat and worn-down boots, creeping from one little obscure shop to another, buying his provisions by the pennyworth. He did not despise coppers now. I have seen him in his garret-room melting gutta-percha in a gallipot, and soleing an old worn pair of boots that a beggar would not have stooped to pick out of the streets—him who once wore the neatest patent leathers, and gave them away to his tiger when there was so much as a crack in the varnish! I have seen him, too, with needle and thread mending his poor coat, and reviving his threadbare trousers with ink. Once I saw him steal into a public-house and purchase a halfpenny-worth of tobacco, which he paid for with two farthings—Shuffleton, who used to smoke cigars at two guineas a pound! Shuffleton, who once took no account of coppers!

Shuffleton's extreme and hopeless poverty places me in a most difficult position in relation to him. In the days of his prosperity, I frequently partook of his splendid hospitality. I was indebted to him for many favours. If I had wanted a five, ten, or twenty-pound note at any time, Shuffleton would have let me have it. In a word, Shuffleton was my very close and intimate friend. But, now, see to what a severe trial he puts my friendship. He has become so shabby that I am ashamed to walk about with him. It would never do for me to hook on to his arm now. Look at his hat, his coat, his boots! What would people say? I should lose by it in my profession. If my companionship did Shuffleton any good, I might be willing to make the sacrifice; but it does not. Shuffleton's arm robs me of that which enriches him not, but makes me, Snobson, look poor indeed. And, in this world of ours, you may as well *be* poor as look poor. All that I can do for Shuffleton is to lend him shillings.

Have I not cause to be angry with Shuffleton for putting himself so far out of the reach of my friendship and sympathy? But Shuffleton is actually angry with me. He reproaches me because I do not visit him more frequently, and throws it in my teeth that I was glad enough to go and see him when he had a good dinner and plenty of wine to give me. This is true, and sounds cutting; but there is no real reproach in it. When Shuffleton, in the days of his prosperity, asked me to stop a week with him, he made no sacrifice whatever. He did not feel the loss of the money I cost him. But he expects me to make a martyr of myself; to ascend two or three times a week to that lofty lodging of his; to sit whole evenings with him, and make believe that I am enjoying myself, while he is engaged with gutta-percha. And when I cannot lend him half a sovereign, he taunts me with ingratitude, and reminds me that formerly he lent me pounds whenever I wanted them. It is hopeless to try and make Shuffleton see that in lending him half a sovereign (when I have one), which I can ill spare, and which he will never repay, I am making a greater sacrifice, and showing more real generosity, than he ever made or showed, when he entertained me for a week, and sent me away with the loan of a ten-pound note. Knowing that Shuffleton is impenetrable to this reasoning, I feel as much hurt as though I were the monster of ingratitude which he believes me to be.

Shuffleton is not the only man who has leagued himself with misfortune to thin the circle of my friends and embitter the joys of my life. There is Idleton. Idleton used to be a smart, presentable, companionable fellow, when he was content to be chief-clerk to a commercial firm in the City. But Idleton became possessed by the insane notion that he was cut out to shine in literature; but the only thing which shines in him in that connection are the knees of his trousers.

I may say, also, that I have no great antipathy to poems in blank verse, and tragedies in five acts, when I meet with them in the printed volume, which I can lay aside when I am weary of it; but, when they are persistently read to me by the author from the original manuscript, whenever I fall in his way, I am bound to own that I have no toleration for them whatever. Since Idleton began to shine in literature, I have taken considerable pains to avoid him. I am changed, he says. I have grown proud. I have forsaken him. What nonsense! It is Idleton who has changed; it is Idleton who has forsaken *me*. Forswear the Muses (and sack), Idleton, indue thyself in a pair of new sixteen shilling trousers, return to the commercial firm in the City, and there's my heart, and there's my hand once more.

The way in which my once valued friend Muddleton plunged headlong into misfortune, merits the utmost rigour of the law. I really think that he loves misfortune. He fairly wallows in it. There is nothing that he seems to like better than to have a severe cold, and be bankrupt and wet through all at once. At the time that I grappled Muddleton to my soul with hooks of steel, he was managing man to Blankton and Co. He never had a cold, nor was bankrupt, nor wet through then. On the contrary, he was the most comfortable dry and solvent man of my acquaintance.

But Muddleton aspired to rule and not to serve. He set up for himself in a damp office in Little Britain, and rheumatism and insolvency became chronic with him from that moment. Now if there be a disastrous speculation to be engaged in anywhere, Muddleton will find it out and engage in it. If there be a shower of rain anywhere, Muddleton is sure to be in it without an umbrella. I never see Muddleton but he is either wet through, or has the marks (particularly on his hat) of having been wet through at some not remote period in the past. I fear that he thinks me ungenerous and unfeeling, because I do not grapple him to my soul as heretofore. How unreasonable! 'Tis he who has unloosed the hooks, not I. Let Muddleton get dry and solvent (a not impossible paradox), and my arms will be open to receive him as of yore. Nay, I will kill the fatted calf and rejoice.

I had a very excellent friend once who turned his back upon me, by letting me and the public know that he had been for years in the habit of robbing a bank: there was another who made himself a stranger to me by obtaining a five-pound note for a distressed widow; and there was a third who separated himself from me (by a vast tract of the ocean), by attaching a signature to a slip of stamped paper.

These be some of the friends who have gone down and left me. Let me mention a few who have gone up and left me. There was Toppleton. Toppleton was one of the oldest and dearest friends I ever had. We were friends in our youth, and we grew up in friendship to manhood. We were inseparable. Toppleton's society was enough for me at any time; my society seemed to be enough for Toppleton. Nothing pleased Toppleton more than to come to my lodging and sit half the night and smoke his pipe and drink his grog, and talk Shakespeare, taste, and the musical-glasses. Nothing pleased me more than to go to Toppleton's lodging and do ditto. We had very little money, either of us; but what we had we shared freely. I have borrowed five shillings of Toppleton many a time, and he has as often borrowed five shillings of me. We concerted many plans for making our fortunes together. Many a time, before parting for the night, have we stood at a corner of a street, and laid out a brilliant future for ourselves.

It is not more than five years since we settled a notable project in this manner, and when we went into a neighbouring tavern to drink success to it, we had only fivepence in coppers between us. It was quite an understood thing that our fortunes should be in common. I have had no quarrel with Toppleton: not an angry word has passed between us; but I would not go to him now and ask him for the loan of five shillings if I were starving. Toppleton has become a rich man. Wealth began to fall upon him in a gentle shower one morning, and (probably while he was thinking of sending for me to take my share of the golden rain) it came on heavier, and poured so hard that he forgot me, I suppose. He came to spend an evening with me, and drank his grog and smoked a cigar. But he no longer talked Shakespeare, taste, and the musical-glasses. He talked Toppleton. An amount of egotism cropped up in his conversation which I had never suspected. It had evidently been a long suppressed conviction of his that Shakespeare was a fool to Toppleton. I did not fall in with this view, and Toppleton and I met less frequently.

We did not, however, part company finally,

until Toppleton mounted a horse. That high horse put a great distance between us immediately. So long as Toppleton walked on foot I could always reach his hand; but now that he was mounted, I was obliged to be content with a wave of the tips of his gloves. O Toppleton, my friend, thou knowest not what pain and anguish, what shame and confusion of face, what soreness of heart thou art causing me! When that golden shower began to fall ever so gently, did I not vow and protest and swear to our acquaintances, by my knowledge of thee, by my friendship for thee, and by my trust in thee, that thou wouldst bear it all meekly and modestly? And now their scoffs and jeers pierce me like arrows.

"How's your friend Toppleton? Has he invited you to dinner in his fine new house, yet?"

I cannot say thou hast, Toppleton.

"The great Toppleton condescended to bow from his brougham to me, to-day."

Such an honour didst thou confer upon me, O Toppleton!

"Lord Toppleton does not look in at the Bearded Oyster, now."

I must own that to be a truth: I never see thee at the Bearded Oyster; and when I called upon you at your chambers the other day, you sent down a message to say that you were busy.

Farewell, Toppleton! may you be happy in that select circle of noodles with which you have encompassed your greatness.

Swellington moved up out of my society in a most absurd manner. It was not a matter of money in his case, but a matter of glossy hat, and gold chain, and slim umbrella, and patent leather boots. All at once Swellington took to being an exquisite. The first thing he did was to part his hair down the middle, shave off his whiskers, and wear a tip and a moustache. Then he took to jewelry, and light kid gloves. I dare say if Middleton and I and the other fellows had followed the movement, we should not have lost the society of Swellington.

But Middleton and I and the other fellows, though always decently clad, are somewhat careless about gloves, and hats, and such matters; and because we walk about with naked hands, and fat umbrellas, and furry hats, Swellington gradually cut us, and took up with another set of fellows, who were more genteel. I know Swellington is not happy among them, for they are an empty-headed set; but then their gloves are all right, and ours are not. I loved Swellington so well that I went to Dent and to Down and made my hands and head all right too, and went up after him; but I found him so much altered for the worse, that I gave him over for good (or evil) to his new associates. Read this in your garret, Shuffleton, and learn how these friends of mine avenge thee.

My friend Middleton has proposed to me to swear eternal friendship. When he made this proposal, I said:

"No, Middleton, don't let us be rash. Suppose that uncle of yours were to die, and leave you his fortune?"

"It wouldn't make the slightest difference in me, my dear boy."

"Don't talk nonsense, my dear Middleton. Your uncle is worth a hundred thousand pounds. If you became possessed of that large sum of money, it would only be natural that you should set up in a fine house, and start your carriage."

"Well, perhaps I might; but that need not alter my friendship for you."

"It will, though."

"Oh, nonsense! How?"

"In this way; you will get into parliament, perhaps."

"Well, possibly."

"And you will become a member of the Reform or the Carlton, where, of necessity, you will spend a good deal of your time."

"Well?"

"Well; I cannot meet you at the Reform or the Carlton."

"But I shall always look in and see my old friends at the Gridiron here."

"No, you won't: it would never do for a Member of Parliament to be seen frequenting a tavern club of this sort. You will have to maintain your position with all things in a concatenation accordingly."

"But I can always ask you to my house."

"Yes; but you won't ask me. You will have to entertain your political friends and others who will swarm about you, and you won't like to introduce your old friend Snobson to lords and cabinet ministers, and right honourables, and grand folks of that sort. You couldn't do it, my dear fellow; it would be absurd."

"I am afraid you are right, Snobson. To put it in the mildest language, we shouldn't see so much of each other as we do now."

"Exactly, Middleton; and if you were to go very much to the bad, it would be the same thing. We shouldn't see so much of each other then. Let's be happy together while we can; but don't let us make any vows."

VERY FREE—AND VERY EASY.

I FONDLY hoped that with the end of September the great invasion would be all over, and that my castle (romantically situated on the heights of Holborn) would be immediately and permanently relieved from occupation by the predatory hordes, which, since May, had from time to time laid siege to it and forced me to surrender.

I was happy in this hope, for though an Englishman's house is undoubtedly his castle, it is still the fate of castles to be assaulted and taken by the enemy; and when the enemy takes the shape of a fat French feuilletonist from Paris, with his still fatter wife; or a Danish drysalter from Copenhagen, with a letter of introduction from the editor of the Schlashbladet; or an American horse-doctor, addicted to expectoration, and a martyr to delirium tremens (kindly recommended by your brother, recently settled in New York); or an old Dublin acquaintance, who never comes home until three o'clock in the morning, and then not sober; or a Scottish chieftain, with no luggage to speak of, who sports his native costume, and collects an admiring audience of spectators round your door every time he goes out, and every time he comes in—when, I repeat, the enemy takes any one of those shapes (not to mention all of them at once), it cannot be said, with any justice, that your castle is any longer *yours.*

I can truly declare that, from the first day of May to the last day of September of the year now happily departed, my castle was not *mine.* It was the fat French feuilletonist's castle, the Danish drysalter's castle, the Scottish chieftain's castle—in fine, I may say it was slave to thousands. It was not until the last of my invaders, the chieftain, took his beak from out my heart, and his picturesque form without my door, and returned to breathe his native air, that I was enabled to breathe *my* native air (albeit getting foggy) with any sense that it was mine, and that I had a title to breathe it.

Reflecting upon all I had suffered, I was still willing to admit that science was a great invention; but, at the same time, I am bound to confess that I considered it a circumstance for congratulation that science (in conjunction with the arts and manufactures) did not hold its jubilee oftener than once in eleven years. I even felt some degree of consolation in the thought that before science, in conjunction with the arts and manufactures, held high festival again, I might be dead, and consequently have no spare bed.

I was revelling in this exhilarating idea one evening somewhere about the tenth of December, when I was startled by a loud knocking at my castle-gate, followed by the sound of a deep-toned and not altogether familiar voice in my hall. Suddenly remembering that several heavy butcher's and other bills for the last quarter were still due, entirely owing to the attractions of science, and the arts and manufactures, I was about to rush out and accept service like a man, when the door of my oak chamber opened suddenly, and there stood before me, attired in a double-caped great-coat, top-boots, and a low-crowned beaver, my old and much-esteemed friend Bovington, of Butterfield, Bucks.

"Here we are," said Bovington.

The way in which Bovington said "Here we are," called up in my mind a sudden vision of Christmas, which, coming in conjunction with the subject of quarterly accounts, gave me a shock. I am afraid I greeted Bovington rather coldly.

"I've come up to see the show," said Bovington, "and mean to stop a week with you."

"Most welcome, I'm sure, Bovington, but

you're a day behind the fair; the Exhibition closed on——"

"Ex-hi-bi-tion!" said Bovington, with measured contempt, "you don't suppose I mean that show. I hate International Exhibitions, bringing over a lot of nasty dirty frog-eating foreigners. I was determined not to come up to London until they were all gone. I mean the Cattle Show."

"Oh, the Cattle Show! To be sure! Well, take off your coat, Bovington, and make yourself comfortable. We'll have supper soon. I dare say you're hungry."

"I could eat a horse," said Bovington.

Those terrible words were scarcely out of Bovington's mouth, when another loud summons at the castle-gate resounded through the hall. I rushed out at once; when who should I see rummaging his pockets for money to pay his cab hire, but my old friend Porkinson, from Sandwich. Porkinson did not see me for a minute, and the first thing I heard him say was, "I've lost a fourpenny-bit."

There immediately flashed across me another vision of Christmas, which was intensified to a most painful degree when Porkinson put his hand in mine, with a slap that resounded all through the castle.

"How are you, my boy? Glad to see you. I told you I'd accept your invitation some day; and now I've done it. Come to stop a day or two with you and see the show."

"Delighted, I'm sure, Porkinson." (I was getting quite cold with joy.) "Let me hang up your coat and things. You will find somebody in there whom you know."

"Shall I, though. Who is it?"

And immediately I heard, "Ha, Bovington!" "What, Porkinson?" followed by a flapping and a slapping that made me think we were really getting up a pantomime, and the comic business had begun.

"Draw up to the fire, Porkinson, and make yourself comfortable. We'll have supper soon. I dare say you're hungry."

"Awful!" said Porkinson; and, as he said so he opened his mouth to that extent that I could see his throat looming in the distance like the entrance to a tunnel. It occurred to me that if Bovington could manage a horse, Porkinson was a likely person to go that entire animal with the addition of a gig. I had serious misgivings about the cold silver-side in the buttery, and I whispered down stairs, "Steaks in quantities, and cut thick."

Bovington, who had all his senses about him

in a preternatural state of working order, overhearing this confidential communication to the regions below, shouted, "And onions."

Bovington and Porkinson are both big and fat and ruddy, and it appeared to me that, as they sat and rubbed their hands, and drew in great draughts of air, they were rapidly exhausting not only my atmosphere but my caloric. My best Wallsend were wholly unequal to the occasion. Bovington and Porkinson seemed to absorb the caloric into themselves as fast as it was generated. They were both in such a state of red-heat, that, when a preliminary half gallon of ale was set before them, it evaporated in a manner suggestive of a clever chemical experiment. Such were their powers of absorption, that I am sure if my banqueting-hall had been adorned with an arseniated paper, Bovington and Porkinson must have fallen victims on the spot; which, I will be candid enough to say, would have been, under the circumstances, a relief.

I was so troubled by these symtoms, that I took an opportunity to slip down into the kitchen to see whether the preparations were on a scale commensurate with the requirements of the case. My mind was somewhat relieved when I found that the steak under treatment closely approximated to the dimensions of the flap of a saddle.

I was in the act of ascending to the chamber where the exhaustive experiments were going on, when another loud knocking at the castle-gate took away my breath, and gave me a stitch in my side. Almost at the same moment the sound of tuneful voices broke upon my ear with

> Oh rest you, merry gentlemen,
> Let nothing you dismay.

"It's the waits?" said Bovington.

"Oh, nonsense," I said, "it's not Christmas yet."

"Jolly Christmas! merry Christmas!" cried Bovington; "I should like to keep Christmas all the year round."

"So should I," said Porkinson, "and have turkey and plum-pudding every day for dinner."

I was far from coinciding in this desire, and proceeded to the door to put a stop to a performance which I felt to be both impertinent and premature.

"Go away, both of you, and don't make this ridiculous noise."

"Ha, ha, ha!" roared a deep thick voice.

"Ho, ho, ho!" echoed another, deep, thick, and loud.

"What? Don't you know me?" said the first.

"Why, bless me," I said, "Puddington!"

"Right you are," said Puddington, "and here's Perkins; both of us come up to stop a day or two with you, and see the beasts. Come in, Perkins. Don't be bashful."

Perkins was not bashful; he came in, and so did Puddington; and Puddington, walking across the hall, sniffed the onions, and said, "Ha!" in a prolonged and hollow manner, which seemed to bode no good to the saddle-flap. Not being even now deserted by my natural politeness, I put it as a probability that Puddington and Perkins were both ready for something to eat.

Puddington said, "I believe you," with an emphasis which placed the sincerity of his avowal beyond question; but Perkins, with a moderation, and, let me add, a modesty, which appeared to me to do equal honour to his head, his heart, and his appetite, merely remarked that he "could peck a bit."

Now I will say that of Puddington, and even of Bovington, and Porkinson, that, when we all five sat down together to the festive board, these three together did not make half the havoc of my silver-side and saddle-flap that Perkins did. Perkins began with cold silver-side, took a turn at hot saddle-flap, and then went back again to silver-side; and had it not been that there were three wooden skewers in the latter, to which I helped him plentifully, I feel certain Perkins would have gone to bed with an appetite. It was a source of great satisfaction to me to observe that Perkins regarded the slices of skewer in the light of horse-radish, and that they appeared to do him good.

"And now," said Bovington, when the cloth was removed, "I'll give you a toast, 'the Queen,' upstanding, gentlemen, and three times three."

The gentlemen stood up, three cheers were duly given, and Bovington's grand (natural) organ pealed forth the key-note of the National Anthem. I was about to protest, even at the risk of incurring the imputation of disloyalty, but the swell of double bass overwhelmed even my power of utterance. The National Anthem was sung to the last verse, and at its conclusion Porkinson said:

"What shall we say after that, Mr Bovington?" To which Mr Bovington solemnly returned:

"Our hearths and homes."

"Hear, hear, hear," by everybody excepting your humble servant, who could not regard *his* hearth and home with any degree of satisfaction under the circumstances.

"Regarding you as the Chair, Mr Bovington, on this auspicious occasion," said Puddington (taking no notice of me, which I considered cool, to say the least of it), "I have to propose, with your permission, the Army and Navy."

"Hear, hear, hear." Drunk with all the honours. Rule Britannia, by Mr Perkins, with full chorus. Sentiment by Mr Perkins: "Britons never will be slaves." "Hear, hear, hear," and thumping of clenched fists on the festive board, expressive of the determination of the company present never to be slaves.

"Mr Chair, if I might be so bold," said Porkinson.

"Gentlemen, gentlemen," I protested.

"I beg your pardon, Simpkins," said Bovington, "but Mr Porkinson is in possession of the chair."

"Hear, hear. Silence for Porkinson."

"Mr Chair and gentlemen," said Mr Porkinson, assuming an attitude that suggested that he had just rendered a signal service to his country, and was standing for his statue—"Mr Chair and gentlemen," Porkinson repeated, "I am about to propose a toast which I am sure will find an echo in every British heart here present—and I believe, Mr Chair, I am justified in saying that all the hearts here present are British—British to the backbone. (Enthusiastic cheers by the vertebrate British hearts.) That being so, Mr Chair,

I will at once propose to you, Our Native Land. (Increased enthusiasm.) It is the land, sir, of—ah—the—ah—brave and the free; it is likewise, as you are well aware, the—ah—pride of the ocean. (Hear, hear.) You have long been acquainted with the fact that Britannia does not require—ah—bulwarks along her shores, but that her path is over the flowing wave, and her home is where the stormy winds do blow upon the mariners of England, who are perfectly indifferent to weather, and whose motto ever is, 'England expects that every man this day will do his dooty.' (Great fervour.) The meteor flag of England, Mr Chair, will ever remind us that—ah—it was in Trafalgar's bay that—ah—we made the Frenchmen belay. Likewise, as regards other bays, including that of Biscay, the prowess of our hearts of oak has been celebrated in songs (mostly with choruses) which will carry the glory of England down to the remotest posterity. (Applause.) The flag to which I have already alluded, Mr Chair, has, as you are aware, braved for a thousand years, and a little over, the battle and the breeze; and while that flag continues to throw over us the—ah—the—"

"Ægis of its protection," suggested Bovington.

"Thank you," continued Porkinson; "while that flag continues to—to do that, why, all I have got to say is, Britons never will be slaves. (Tumultuous approbation.) Sir; we have reason to be proud of our native land; and particularly we have reason to be proud of ourselves. (Hear, hear.) I mean as Englishmen. As Englishmen, sir, we are superior to the whole human race. What are foreign nations to compare with us? Take any one of them you like. What are Frenchmen? What are they? Why a miserable set of skillygolee-fed mountebanks. One Englishman can thrash a dozen Frenchmen any day—ah, and eat 'em too! (Great applause, and Hear, hear, from Perkins.) Take your Germans, again—a squad of undersized, mouldy-cheeked, square-backed, whity-brown, sour-krout-eating louts. (Prolonged cheers.) And your Italians—set of beggars and caterwauling opera-singers. As for Spain, sir, I don't believe there is an individual in that benighted country who is fit to do anything but smoke paper cigars and drive a donkey. (Cheers and laughter.) Now why is it that these foreign nations are so benighted and besotted and ignorant, and so generally inferior to Englishmen? Why is it? I'll tell you why; because they 've got no stomachs! Give a Frenchman a pound of good beefsteak such as that we have partaken of this evening—"

I ventured upon the correction, "Rump."

"Rump, was it?" Mr Porkinson continued. "Very well; give a Frenchman a pound of good rump-steak, and what will he do with it? Why, he will boil it down in a gallon of water, and drink it out of a teacup. (Cheers.) Give a Spaniard a pipe of good strong shag tobacco to smoke, and what does it do to him?"

"Makes him sick," suggested Perkins.

"Exactly," said Porkinson; "and do you mean to tell me that people like that are worthy to be free and have equal laws, and all that sort of thing? (No! no!! NO!!!) And why are Englishmen superior to them? *Be*cause they have got stomachs. Because they can put away a pound of steak per man without winking. I have no hesitation in saying that it is the roast beef of Old England that has won us our liberties. Do you imagine that the barons could have induced King John to sign Magna Charta had they met him after a dinner of skilly? Never! King John, sir, would have seen them hanged first. And where, but for the roast beef of Old England, where, I should like to know, would have been Habeas Corpus? (Cries of Nowhere, and thunders of applause.) Therefore, Mr Chair, I give you Our Native Land, the land of liberty and freedom, the land of just and equal laws, the land of security to property and protection to the subject—in fact, sir, our own, our native land." (Enthusiastic outburst of approbation, after which, Home, sweet Home, by Mr Perkins.)

Sentiment: "England, home, and beauty."

Supplementary song by Mr Puddington, the Red, White, and Blue.

Sentiment: "May the present moment be the worst of our lives."

Attempted additional vocal effort by Perkins, but suspended in the middle of the second verse, owing to defective memory, the whole concluding with a general getting up-stairs (with difficulty) to bed, to the tune of Rule Britannia, mingled with God save the Queen, the Brave Old Oak, the Maids of Merry England, and Wapping Old Stairs; the last suggested to the facetious Perkins by the creaking of my ancestral timbers.

I pass a troubled night, with Britannia sitting on my chest, and beating time to commingled patriotic choruses with the end of her trident, and awake abruptly to the reality of Bovington thundering at my door, with the information that it is time for breakfast. After a hurried toilet I arrive in the banqueting-hall, to find Bovington, Puddington, Porkinson, and Perkins rubbing their hands and chafing for food, in a manner highly suggestive of the Zoological Gardens on a Saturday at three. With as little delay as possible I endeavour to appease the appetite of the lion, Bovington, with a lump of fried beef; to the Bengal tiger, Porkinson, I throw a grilled fowl; before the hippopotamus, Puddington, I scatter a panful of potatoes and frizzled bacon; and into the den of the boa-constrictor, Perkins, I cast a great blanket of ham omelette. There is much growling and gnashing and snarling and beating of bars, and then there is nothing; and to my infinite relief Bovington, Porkinson, Puddington, and Perkins rise to take their departure for the day. And as Bovington is putting himself into his double-caped top-coat, he says:

"What time do you dine, old fellow?"

"Ah, to be sure," says Porkinson. "What's your hour?"

With faltering accents I mention the hour of six.

"All right," says Bovington; "I'll be here."

And Porkinson, Puddington, and Perkins all express the same resolve in the most assuring manner.

"And now, gentlemen," says Bovington, "I'll tell you what my plans are for the day. I mean first of all to visit the Cattle Show; then I shall go to the Tower, and see the crown jewels; after that I shall come up the river and view the Houses of Parliament, the Queen's palace, and the palace of the Archbishop of Canterbury; and finally, I shall look into the British Museum, and inspect the original Magna Charta, which I am told is preserved in the manuscript department. Now, if you, gentlemen, approve this plan, we may as well all go together; and if we part company or lose each other, why, we shall all meet again round Simpkins's hospitable board at six."

Mr Bovington's programme met with general approval, the places he mentioned being exactly those which Porkinson, Puddington, and Perkins, as true Britons, proud of their country and its glorious institutions, desired above all things to see. So Bovington, Porkinson, Puddington, and Perkins went forth to view the national lions.

With a full knowledge of the programme of proceedings which my visitors had chalked out for themselves, I was somewhat surprised by the sudden and unexpected return of Perkins at noon.

"I dare say you wonder to see me back so soon," said Perkins, emerging from a cab, carefully carrying some large and apparently fragile article, elaborately wrapped up in brown paper; "but the fact is, I met with a bargain, and I thought I'd better bring it home myself, in case of accidents."

"What is it, Perkins?"

"A magnificent or-molu and china clock,"

said Perkins; "bought it a great bargain at an auction in the Strand; just the very thing I wanted for my drawing-room mantel-shelf. It's really a splendid clock, and dirt cheap at four pounds."

Mr Perkins was quite flushed with exultation, and cut the twine and tore off the brown paper which enshrouded his treasure with nervous impatience.

"Halloa!" he exclaimed, suddenly.

"What's the matter?" I asked.

"Why," said Perkins, "this is not the clock I bought!"

"Not the clock?"

"No, I should think not; look at it; all the gilding worn off, the glass cracked, and one of the hands wanting."

"Well, it is not a very magnificent affair, Perkins; and at four pounds, I think is rather dear."

"Rather dear! I should think so. There's some mistake, or else I've been shamefully cheated. But I'll not be done. I'll take it back, and if they don't give me the clock I bought and paid for, I shall apply to a magistrate."

"I certainly should, if I were you."

"I shall, you may depend upon it," said Perkins; and with that he wrapped up his bargain, and was off in another cab to the Strand.

Perkins had not been long gone when the servitor entered to say that a person wanted to see me.

"Who is the person?"

"He didn't give his name, sir; but he says he comes from the hospital."

"The hospital! Who can he be? What can he want?"

On being introduced, the person explained that he had been sent from the hospital to inform me that a gentleman had been brought in there in a state of insensibility, and that, on searching his pockets, a card had been found, bearing my name and address. The two ideas which this information called up in my mind were Bovington and apoplexy, succeeded immediately by a vision of Puddington and paralysis, dissolving as quickly into a view of Perkins in a fit.

As the messenger could give me no further information, I hurried to the hospital, to learn the terrible truth for myself. It was Puddington! At the moment of my arrival he was under treatment with the stomach-pump. Presently it was announced that he had recovered his senses, and I was admitted to see him. The pallor which overspread Puddington's countenance I should not have thought possible.

"Halloa, Puddington! What's happened, old fellow?"

When Puddington had collected his scattered senses a little, he whispered in reply, "Skittles!" and, on being questioned further, murmured of "old ale;" and then babbled vaguely of his "watch and money."

Puddington soon recovered himself, and I took him home in a cab, and placed him in an arm-chair by the side of the fire.

"Cheer up, Puddington," I said; "Bovington, and Porkinson, and Perkins will be here shortly, and we'll have dinner, and you'll soon be all right, and sing us a song."

These words of consolation were scarcely out of my mouth when I heard the accents of Porkinson—loud and angry—in the hall. The next instant Porkinson entered in great excitement, with his face flushed, an ugly mark about his eye, his hat smashed, and his coat torn.

"Why, bless me, Porkinson, what's happened?"

"Happened!" said Porkinson; "look at that and look at this."

"That," referred to a small photograph; "this," to Porkinson.

"Do you call that a likeness?" said Porkinson, with indignation.

"Well, it is certainly not a very pleasing one."

"I should think not," said Porkinson; "and because I declined to pay for it, and insisted upon having another done, the ruffian photographer hit me a blow in the eye; his wife, a perfect fury, seized me by the hair of the head; and their miscreant of a son hung on to my coat-tails and kicked my shins; and all this in a public thoroughfare, in broad day, in the nineteenth century; and the police declined to take them in charge."

"This is what I call shameful—disgraceful. I couldn't have believed such a thing possible—in a free country."

These words broke in upon us from the hall, while Porkinson was still giving vent to his indignation, and the next instant Perkins entered with a brown-paper parcel.

"They won't change it, and I can get no redress. It's a regular den of cheats and thieves. I was hustled out of the place, and when I applied to the magistrate, he told me I must sue them in the County Court. Look at the thing," continued Perkins; "I find now that it hasn't got a pendulum. And what do you think? I am told the auction is a mock one, a sham and a snare; and yet in this free country there is no law to put it down!"

"Oh, please, sir; please, sir!"

"What's the matter now?" I asked of the breathless servitor, who arrived on the distressing scene with these words of foreboding.

"The police, sir, with somebody in custody."

"The police! Somebody in custody! Do they take this for a station house?"

I rush to the door, and find two policemen on the step holding up a stout gentleman (with difficulty) between them. The light from the hall-lamp showed me the swollen face of Bovington.

"Why, what has happened? Is he dr——?"

"No, sir; not that. The gent's had the misfortune to be garotted."

"Garotted!"

"Yes, sir. Found him lying on the pavement near the British Museum. He's been robbed, sir, and rather ill treated."

When Bovington was brought in and placed in an arm-chair opposite Puddington, the sight of him with his swollen face and protruding eyes, as if they had nearly been squeezed out of him, was so pitiful, that Porkinson and Perkins were fain to subside into silence.

I regret to say that when the sirloin came up, the only one of the party who had any appetite for old English fare was Perkins. Bovington, Porkinson, and Puddington begged to be excused from drawing up to the table, and sat by the fire with basins on their knees, and partook of soup. It would have been a very melancholy party indeed, especially after the hilarity of the night before, had not my entertaining neighbour, Monsieur Petitpoint, the music-master, stepped in to cheer us with his lively talk.

"Ah! what you say?" exclaimed M. Petitpoint; "all your friends hockust, garotted, sheated, boxed, ponched on ze head—all in a day, and in ze broad daylight! Ah, parbleu, zat is very bad!"

"It *is* bad," I said; "but my friend Mr Bovington's case is the worst. He had been into the British Museum to see the original document of Magna Charta——"

"Magna Charta!" exclaimed M. Petitpoint; "ah ze grand sharter of English leeberty! We have no such sing as zat in France—zere is no such sing as zat in ze whole world—only in ze Grand Bretagne!"

"Yes, exactly, M. Petitpoint; but Mr Bovington had scarcely got outside the Museum—at four o'clock in the afternoon—when a ruffian seized him by the throat, while another rifled his pockets, and then threw him with violence on the pavement."

"Ah, parbleu!" exclaimed M. Petitpoint,

"but we have not zat in France, in ze broad day. But nevaire you mind, Monsieur Bovington," continued the lively Petitpoint, patting my guest upon the back; "you have a great nassion! you have leeberty! you have juistees! And, look you, I shall play you my last composission wid all ze beautiful arias of your grand nassion." With that, M. Petitpoint lighted a cigarette, sat down to the piano, and, with exquisite good nature and lightness of heart, played a grand fantasia, embracing God save the Queen, Rule Britannia, the Red, White, and Blue, and I don't know how many national and patriotic airs besides.

The effect of this music—but especially of Rule Britannia—on my swindled and half-murdered guests, was highly stimulating; indeed, they began within half an hour to patronize, protect, and pity M. Petitpoint, and to offer to accompany *him* to the British Museum to inspect Magna Charta, and take his chance of being garotted at the gate. But for myself I must confess, that, although my waistcoat expanded under the influence of Rule Britannia, as it invariably does, still I caught myself unpatriotically wishing that Britannia would rule her scoundrels a little better. I admit that it is charming, logical, and unanswerable, to sing Rule Britannia on all occasions for the demolition of all grumblers, and moral extinction of all foreigners; but if, as to her ruffian population, Britannia would try her shield a little less, and her trident (getting it ground for the purpose) a little more, would she rule us *much* the worse? As one who decidedly never never never will—if he can help it—I suggest the question. Britons are very free, but need they be so very easy too?

MY PANTOMIME.

Let me repeat what I have already been privileged to state in these pages, that there is nothing of which I am more thoroughly convinced than that I, the writer of this article, was born a poet.* And when I say poet, I desire it to be understood that I do not mean a mere jingler of rhymes, but the real article, fine frenzied as to eye, and turned-down as to collar. It is of very little consequence to me, whether you, the reader, believe this or not. *I* believe it, and that is enough for my feelings under the heart-rending circumstances I am about to relate. Think of this; think of the poet, your most devoted servant, with this conviction at his breast, and a five-act tragedy in his pocket, being waited upon by the manager of a theatre, and asked to write a Pantomime! Imagine Moses and Son waiting upon Alfred Tennyson with a commission for an ode upon Trousers!

This is where the sting lay: I had spoken to the manager about my tragedy; I had given it him to read; he had read it—at least he said so

* See Tragic Case of a Comic Writer, page 1.

—and sent it back with the opinion and decision that it was an excellent tragedy, but would not do for his establishment. Then a month or two afterwards, within a very short time of Christmas, he comes to my humble abode in his carriage, and says:

"My dear sir, I want you to write my Christmas Pantomime."

Once more call up, in your mind, Moses making his bow and his request in the study of the Laureate. I was shocked, hurt, wounded in my tenderest part. Write a Pantomime? I! I! In my attic chamber I felt as indignant as Andrew Marvel is said to have felt when he declared his préference for cold mutton and virtue in Maiden-lane, to whitebait and wickedness in Whitehall.

"Sir, I have the heel of a Dutch cheese and half of a penny loaf in my cupboard, and——"

I had got thus far in the preparation of a withering and indignant reply to the degrading proposal, when the manager interposed:

"You see, my dear sir, I am in a difficulty. Syllabus, who usually does my Pantomime, has two others on his hands this year. He has the Lane and the Garden to write, and so he shows his gratitude to the man who made him, by leaving me in the lurch. The scenery and properties are ready, and all I want is the opening. You must do it."

"I! I! Mr Maberly."

Mr Maberly said, emphatically, "You."

"What on earth, Mr Maberly, made you think of me for such a task?"

"What made me think of *you*, my dear fellow?—why, your tragedy!"

"My tragedy!"

"Yes; I read it—did, upon my honour—and before I got through the first act, I said to myself, 'This is the man to do my Pantomime; his style is exactly the thing.'"

Was it for this that I had devoted my days and nights to the study of the immortal bard? Was it for this that I had made a pilgrimage (in a very indifferent pair of boots) to his shrine! How I restrained myself from committing an act of violence I do not know; but I did, and I said with terrible calmness:

"Sir, have you come hither to insult me?"

"On the contrary," said Mr Maberly, "I have come here to do you a service. Look here, now; you are a youngster; you have never had a piece produced. You want an introduction. I am prepared to give you one. Write my Pantomime; your name will appear in the bills; the papers and the public will speak of you, and there you are at once, a dramatic author, with the market open to you."

Beginning to perceive that Mr Maberly really meant well by me, I said sadly, "I had other views."

"I know you have," said Mr Maberly; "you aim at the high-flown sort of thing, tragedy, five-act comedy, and so forth. But, my dear sir, you must creep before you can walk; walk before you can run. Begin with pantomime, then try comedy, and no doubt in the course of time you will arrive at tragedy. Edmund Kean, sir, played harlequin before he attempted Richard. Garrick occasionally wrote his own pantomimes. Beginners should not be too particular; take my advice, and accept the gifts the gods provide you; I can assure you there is nothing the gods are so partial to, as a good pantomime."

Mr Maberly's eloquence and persuasive reasoning were gradually undermining the foundations of my lofty aspirations. Garrick had written pantomimes, Edmund Kean had played harlequin; and here was an offer of thirty pounds for 600 lines of doggrel verse. Well, there was no harm in doing what Garrick had done, and thirty pounds was more than the great Johnson got for Irene. I consented.

But I stooped only to conquer in the end. I

resolved that the Pantomime should be the thin end of the wedge, and that I should eventually rend the deep-rooted tree of prejudice and debased taste by the thick end of blank verse and five acts.

"Very well," said Mr Maberly, "here is the scene-plot, and I may tell you that the scenes are all settled, and most of them painted, and you must manage your story to fit them."

I ventured to express some surprise at this arrangement, which appeared to me a good deal like putting the cart before the horse. Mr Manager, however, gave me to understand that in the matter of Pantomime, and, indeed, even in the case of drama, he regarded the scene-painter as the horse, and the author as the cart.

"No disrespect to you, sir, but in these days there's nothing like scenery. The best of your craft require the scene-painter to pull you through. Don't suppose for a moment that I approve of this state of things. Why should I? What do I give you for the piece? Thirty pounds! But the transformation scene, with the flying fairies, costs me a couple of hundred. If pens, ink, and paper, were as dear as wood, paint, and canvas, I couldn't afford to pay for authorship at all. I should have to gag it; and 'pon my word, sir, without any disrespect to you, I think I should get on just as well."

Insult upon injury! but I bore it calmly, and said, "I think, sir, you mentioned something about the story of the piece?"

"Ah, yes, to be sure, the story; I was nearly forgetting that. Let me see; everything's been done so, and new things are hazardous. After all, there's nothing like one of the good old nursery tales; everybody knows the names of them. What do you say to Jack the Giant Killer?"

I said I thought it had been used very often.

"Yes, so it has; well, Mother Hubbard?"

"That has been done also, and very lately."

"True; the year before last. Then Red Riding Hood. But now I remember that was done last year. Everything's been done, that's the fact. Never mind; I'll tell you what we'll do. We'll combine two or three of them, and make up for the lack of what is new by a liberal abundance of what is old. So let us say; Harlequin Jack the Giant Killer; or, Old Mother Hubbard, Little Red Riding Hood, and the Field of Forty Footsteps. There's nothing new now-a-days but combinations, and there you have one;—though by the way, you might give it a little dash of originality by making the number of footsteps fifty instead of forty. The alliteration is quite as good, and it shows a disposition on the part of the management to give as much as possible for the money. Now, set to work, there's a good fellow; I shall expect the last scene in by Saturday week."

"One word, sir, before you go. I don't quite see my way to the—the combination."

"Not see your way to the combination?"

"Well, not exactly; how am I to connect Mother Hubbard with Jack?"

"Nothing more easy. Make her his mother —or, stop; say grandmother if you can get more fun out of her that way."

"And Little Red Riding Hood, sir?"

"Jack's sister, of course; or his sweetheart; which you like."

"And the Field of Forty Footsteps?"

"Oh, well, if you can't manage that, make it The Thirteen Thieves, or anything that will fit and look new. Good morning. I shall expect you to read on Saturday week, before treasury; not after, mind. Actors can't listen to anything with a whole week's salary in their pockets."

And I, a poeta nascitur, was left to contemplate the scene-plot of Harlequin Jack the Giant Killer; or, Old Mother Hubbard, Little Red Riding Hood, and the Field of Forty Footsteps, and to fill it up with doggrel rhymes and jingling puns. I went to the drawer and looked at my tragedy in sorrow and in shame, with iron at my soul and fetters upon my hands, for I was tied and bound in the service of Momus. I took my tragedy out and read a portion of it. When I came to where Cromwell bids them "take away that bauble," I felt that the words were a reproach to myself. There was *my* bauble lying on the table, in the shape of the scene-plot of a Pantomime. I put "Oliver Cromwell in five acts" away, and dragged myself in my chains to my table. I sat down to write: "Scene First. —Cottage of Old Mother Hubbard. Mother Hubbard preparing breakfast. Jack asleep in bed." It was a long time before I got any further; but at length, after much excogitation, I succeeded in hammering out the opening scene. I read it over to myself aloud. Whether it was in the dialogue, or in the manner of reading it, I don't know, but it seemed to me that the opening scene of my Pantomime sounded very like the opening scene of my tragedy. Mother Hubbard's admonition to Jack was quite in the vein of Queen Henrietta's address to her son, Prince Charles.

I began to see that I was not equal to the task I had undertaken. My key was a deal too high. But how was I to lower it, to unscrew it down to the proper pitch? I had no books of Pantomimes to read and study, and of course there were no Pantomimes being played in November that I could go and see. In looking through the theatrical advertisements in the papers, however, I saw that a burlesque was running at one of the houses. That was as near an approach to a Pantomime as I could have. I resolved to go that very evening and study it. I went and sat for two hours in the front row of the pit, with my chin resting on the back of the orchestra, and my eyes fixed on the stage. I studied the method attentively and minutely, and, with the puns and parodies ringing in my ears, went home to write.

With an entirely new inspiration I re-wrote the scene between Jack and his mother, and this time it was not so like the tragedy. Still it seemed to be wanting in the breadth and familiarity of expression which characterized my model. For example, I had made Mother Hubbard bid Jack "shake seductive slumber from his eyes," and also inform him that "Labour awaited him at the garden gate," expressions which were undoubtedly neat, but not by any means of the gaudy character which becomes a Pantomime. A friend of great experience calling on me while I was struggling with this difficulty, recommended the use of the slang dictionary, and kindly lent me a copy. The study of this work enabled me to make great improvements in my MS. Thus for "eyes," I wrote "peepers;" for "head," "nut;" for "hands," "mawleys;" and where any one was told to vanish or go away, I substituted "hook it," or "walk your chalks." When I had made these and similar alterations, my friend declared that the dialogue was much funnier; though he thought it might be still further improved by a little peppering here and there. By peppering I understood him to mean the insertion of puns, and I flattered myself that I had introduced a good many very excellent puns already. "Ah! my dear fellow," said my friend and counsellor, "that's where you make the mistake. Your puns are too good. It's the bad ones that tell. Here, for example, you have

"'*Jack.* Mother, a great long ogre's at the door.

"'*Mother Hub.* A great long ogre, say you? That's a bore.'

"That's not bad, certainly; but it is too tame for the highly educated taste of the present day. Put it in this way, for example:

"'*Mother Hub.* You must be wrong.

"'*Jack.* No; 'twas a great long ogre.

"'*Mother Hub.* O, g'long.'"

"Excuse me," I said, "but I don't quite see the——"

"Not see it! Long ogre—o, g'long. The sound, according to the pronunciation, is precisely the same."

"Yes, but the sense?" I said.

"Sense! If you stick at sense you will never succeed in this branch of literature."

Acting upon this friendly advice, I set to work to pepper my production with puns after the approved model. I am bound to confess that it was hard work, and I soon began to perceive that it was absolutely necessary in many instances—indeed in most—to change the natural subject of the dialogue entirely, in order to introduce them. For instance, finding the word "opportunity" in a speech, and endeavouring to pun upon it, I arrived at "hop-or-two-nity," and *h*opera-tune-ity." Now, as neither the act of hopping, nor the subject of opera tunes, properly belonged to the theme, I was obliged to drag them in neck and heels. I am quite willing to confess that the tragedy never gave me half so much trouble. There I was, all day long, hunting through Johnson's Dictionary for words to pun upon; and, oftener than not, when I had twisted them about, and turned them upside down and inside out upon slips of paper, no pun would come of it, and I had to take another word and repeat the same process. Possibly you are not aware what it is to go to bed and dream of puns, and beat the devil's tattoo on the counterpane in the effort to produce couplets.

The manager called several times to see how I was getting on. I read the scenes to him, and he was pleased to say they would "do." He did not bestow any higher praise; candidly confessing that he made it a point never to praise a piece until he saw how it went with the audience, and what the newspapers said of it. Even then, he was not disposed to be extravagantly eulogistic, unless he found full warranty for so being, in the treasury.

At the appointed time I proceeded to the theatre to read the piece to the company. I had long looked forward to that bright day; but, now that it had come, it was not so bright as my fervid fancy had painted it. I had pictured myself in a pillared and curtained apartment reading to lofty-mannered tragedians assembled in solemn conclave. I found myself in a little dark mouldy room, in the midst of a throng of low comedians, and singing chamber-maids, and acrobats, and ballet-dancers, who paid me no respect whatever, but regarded me with marked suspicion and distrust. I read the piece amid dead silence. No one condescended to laugh but the leader of the orchestra; and the low comedian told me immediately afterwards that that was a very bad omen, for it was proverbial in theatres that when the orchestra gave a pre-judgment of approval, the piece was almost certain to be damned.

The grave and solemn looks with which all the actors slunk out of the room after the reading, made me very uneasy, until the prompter assured me that they always did that, and made it a rule never to express their opinion of a piece until the parts were given out. The only encouraging face that I had noticed among the company, belonged, as I found, to the pantaloon, who, on my timidly asking him what he thought of my production, said:

"Oh! it will do very well, I dare say; but you see the people at this house don't listen much to the opening: they're always impatient for the comic business."

The "comic business," I was given to understand, meant the harlequinade, as distinguished from the introductory dialogue, which was not regarded (from a professional point of view) as comic. On one point my friend the pantaloon expressed a very decided opinion: The piece was too long.

"The people here, you see, sir, usually whistle through the opening. When they get tired of whistling, they shy ginger-beer bottles, and pull up the seats. Take my advice, sir, and cut it."

When the parts had been given out, and the actors had assembled on the stage for rehearsal, I found that the young lady who played Jack, and the low comedian who played the Giant (on stilts), and the second old man who played Mother Hubbard (in petticoats), differed from the pantaloon in toto. The young lady came up to me and, in an imperative manner, said, her part must be "written up," or she would certainly not play it. She was such a pretty and engaging little lady, that I said I would do anything to oblige her; but when I spoke to the manager about it, he said she *must* play the part or leave the theatre; and when I told this to the little lady, she said I was a nasty disagreeable man, and that I might have written up her part without saying a word to the manager.

The leading low comedian, whom I felt proud to meet and know, assumed a hostile attitude towards me at once. On being introduced, he was willing to shake hands with me, and hope I was quite well; but he clearly gave me to understand that amenities could go no further while his part remained as it was. His complaint was, that his part was a great deal too short, and that all the best lines were given to Jack. What he wanted me to do, was, to write his part up, and give him all Jack's good lines.

I should have been most willing to oblige the leading low comedian to the full extent of my ability; but to ask Jack to give up her pet lines was more than I dared do. From what I had already seen of Jack, I felt justified in the belief that she would have met any proposition of the kind with a hostile demonstration of physical force. The second old man (owing, as I subsequently understood, to the smallness of his salary, and consequently of his importance in the theatre) did not venture upon direct protest, but talked *at* me, shrugging his shoulders, and saying to other malcontents, loud enough for me to hear, that he was afraid his health would break down under so much study.

In my imagination, I had always pictured a stage rehearsal as a very pleasant affair. Realizing it, I found that, as the author, I was regarded as an enemy by every one who had a part in the piece; and that I had not only made all the actors inimical to myself, but to each other. The leading low comedian and the leading young lady had been on the best terms possible until I sowed the seeds of discord between them by providing them respectively with the parts of Jack, and the Giant. Jack confided to me privately that, so far as the lines were concerned, she would much rather have been the Giant; while the Giant protested, for the same reason, that he would have infinitely preferred to be Jack. There was only one point on which they were unanimous, and that was in their hatred of me, and their envy of each other.

The discontent of these two was so unreasonable that I could treat it with indifference; but it cut me to the quick to be pitifully informed by the second old man, whom I had been partly instrumental in casting for Mother Hubbard, that his line of business, until he had joined that theatre, had been tragedy, and that he had been accustomed to enact Macbeth and Coriolanus. I had a fellow-feeling for the second old man, and could have sympathized with him, if he had only been commonly civil. But he would insist on altering my couplets and introducing "gags," which I could not approve. Thus, without any rhyme or reason whatever, he persisted in substituting for a very neat joke, the vulgar expression: "Hollo, boys, there goes another guy!" which he said was safe to bring the house down.

The Giant also took similar liberties, and

finished lines with, "What's your little game?" "Who's your hatter?" "How's your poor feet?" and other slang expressions of the streets, which had no relation whatever to the subject of the dialogue. I protested that I could not allow my name to appear in connection with such nonsense, and begged the Giant to speak only the words set down for him. I had my reputation to study. The Giant retorted that *he* had his reputation to study too; and he had the audacity to say that there was not a laugh in the whole piece, and that, unless he was permitted to do something to "hit the people up," it would be damned.

I had prided myself particularly upon my happy selection of music, and the neatness of my parodies. Judge of the outrage to my feelings, when Jack declined to sing Come where my Love lies Dreaming, and insisted upon Skid-a-ma-link, with a comic dance. Jack carried her point, and this encouraged the Giant to reject the King of the Cannibal Islands, which was highly appropriate, in favour of I wish I was with Nancy, which was apropos of nothing; there being no Nancy in the piece, and no reason for the Giant wishing himself anywhere but where he was. I flattered myself that there could be no earthly objection to my effective parody of the grand scena from Sonnambula; but the unanimous voice of all concerned declared for the Perfect Cure, with a jumping accompaniment. I had been patient and forbearing hitherto; but this was too much. I appealed against the Perfect Cure to the manager.

"My dear sir," was the manager's reply, "don't say a word against the Cure. It's a safe card—always goes. We had a farce not long ago that was on the high road to ruin. The people began to goose it, five minutes after the curtain was up: they goosed it all through. What did I do? I went to the wing and whispered to the cast to dance the Cure. They did, and it saved the piece. The curtain fell amid a storm of applause, and the Cure was encored."

The manager had previously expressed himself thus:

"Lord bless you, sir, when we have played it for a night or two you won't know it again." This was verified before it was played at all, and I retired from the last rehearsal in disgust, to find the clown and pantaloon in their practising dresses at the wing, impatiently fretting and fuming at the long time taken over the "lingo." This was the contemptuous epithet those worthies applied to that opening which had cost me days of toil, and nights of torture.

In the midst of my humiliation, I had but one

consolation. The piece would make me a dramatic author, and, as Mr. Maberly said, introduce me to the market. I thought with hope of my neglected tragedy in the drawer at home.

Boxing night came, and the curtain rose upon Harlequin Jack the Giant Killer; or, Old Mother Hubbard, Little Red Riding Hood, and the Field of Fifty Footsteps. I sat in a corner of the dress-circle with feelings of mingled shame and dread. I felt like a criminal in the dock, conscious of his crime, and fearfully awaiting the verdict. In my anxiety I had no ears for the words, and the first thing that attracted my attention was a round of applause. I anxiously inquired of my next neighbour what the actor had said to excite so much enthusiasm? His reply was,

"What's your little game?" and he said it through his laughter, as if he thought it a very good point indeed. Another roar succeeded, and this time I heard for myself the joke which was so much approved. It was Mother Hubbard's exquisite witticism of "Hollo, boys, there goes another guy!" At this point, a friend came round to congratulate me.

"It's going capitally," he said; "the audience have taken it from the first, and you will see it will be all right;" and he patted me on the shoulder encouragingly. My face was like a burning coal. I could have wished the dress-circle to open and let me quietly into the earth. My own pet jokes and neatly-turned witticisms scarcely excited a smile, except from some undemonstrative people in the stalls, who were too genteel to applaud.

My friend evidently took the redness of my face for the flush of triumph: it was the crimson of shame. But what could I say? Was not the piece, as he said, going capitally? When the Giant said, "How's your poor feet!" a yell of delight burst from the audience. As for the "Cure," it was encored twice, and the applause continued for several minutes, and was perfectly deafening. My friend came round again to slap me decisively on the shoulder, and say I was a made man.

My success was too much for me; and, amid a storm of applause caused by Jack (entirely on his own responsibility) asking the Giant "where he was going on Sunday?" I fled from the intoxicating scene, and went forth to cool my fevered brain. Presently I found myself behind the scenes, the storm of applause raging more fiercely than ever. It was the end of the opening, and the transformation scene was on. There was a call. It was for the manager, in acknowledgment of the amount of gold-leaf he had lavished upon the Dell of Delight. There was another call. It was for the artist who had designed the Dell of Delight, and spread the gold-leaf which the manager had paid for. There was a third call. It was for the author, and I plainly heard the voice of my friend above all the others, and leading them.

I muttered to myself "Never!" but the manager came up at that moment, and, pushing me towards the curtain, said, "Go on! go on!"

I had no time to resist. The prompter pulled back the curtain, told me sharply to take off my hat, the manager gave me a shove, and there I was on the stage bowing to the public.

Ah, little did I dream then that I was bowing my neck in the dust to be trampled upon and degraded! Next morning the critics were loud in their praises of my Pantomime. It "sparkled with puns and parodies and smart allusions to the topics of the day, and kept the audience in a roar of laughter from beginning to end." As for the author, he was congratulated on the circumstance that he would wake that morning and find himself famous *as a writer of Pantomime.* Other writers in the same department were warned to look to their laurels.

I must confess that it was with a sense of triumph that I read this. Not that I was proud of my Pantomime. But I was now a dramatic author, and the market was open to me. Now for my tragedy!

I took the earliest opportunity of trying the market with that commodity. I offered it right and left. No one would have it. Not that the article was not in demand; but no one would buy of *me*. "My dear sir, tragedy is not in your line; stick to pantomime, that is your forte."

"Tragedy! My dear fellow, oh, nonsense; if you have got a good short, smart, rattling farce now—"

Such was the invariable reply; and such has been the reply to this hour, whenever I have proposed to do any work of a higher order than a pantomime, a farce, or a comic sketch. Yet I am a poet. I could prove it if I could only find an editor to insert my verses. What was the reply the other day when I proposed a paper on the Sublimation of Thought as exemplified in the Philoctétes of Sophocles? This:

"I am rather afraid of that subject; suppose you write something about the Pantomime—which is more in your line." Well; here it is.

CUPID'S MANUFACTORY.

THE name and address of the eminent manufacturing firm of Cupid and Co. are not to be found in the Post-office Directory. I know this because I have searched the magnum opus through all its divisions without being able to discover them. Nevertheless, the firm has not only a name but a local habitation; and I have visited the habitation, been over the works, and know all about the concern. I have long aspired to possess this knowledge. Years past, when, long before the advent of the month which is popularly supposed to usher in the mating season of both birds and men, I have noticed the windows of small booksellers and stationers break out into a pictorial rash in anticipation of the Feast of St Valentine, I have been in the habit of wondering how and where the outbreak originated.

With regard to such matters I can claim a certain community of mind with his deceased Majesty King George the Third. When I see apple-dumplings I am very curious to know how the apples found their way inside the dumplings.

So, for years, I was anxious to know where the valentines came from; who executed those highly-coloured illustrations of a lady and gentleman walking arm and arm up a pale brown pathway towards a salmon-coloured church in the immediate vicinity (the lady and gentleman being considerably taller than the church); who wrote that beautiful poetry where "love" is for ever sweetly linked with "dove," save occasionally when it spoils the rhyme by a disposition to "rove," or retire into a "grove," and where "twine" is so largely employed in the penultimate lines as to convey the idea that the poet ran his poetry off a reel and made it up in balls; who printed them, who coloured them, who stuck Cupids and transfixed hearts upon them; how, in fact, they found their way into those shop windows, to be offered to an affectionate public at prices varying from one farthing up to two pound two?

I have been to the mint, and, having seen love's tokens coined, I am now about to describe the process. No matter how I discovered the mint; suffice it that, from information I received, I proceeded there, and found Cupid and Company actively engaged in their business, on extensive premises situate in Love-lane, number thirty-five. Perhaps you are unacquainted with Love-lane;

may never have heard of it before. Well,—no matter; if you should ever go there, you will find it remarkably like Red Lion-square. Paint the picture how you will, you cannot make anything but a red lion of it. However, Love-lane is better, as it gets rid of an unpleasant association with the Mendicity Society, an idiot asylum, and several forlorn institutes, with dirty door-steps and cobwebbed windows.

The outside of Cupid's manufactory is perhaps a little disenchanting to the visitor, who has been drawing fancy pictures of it in his mind coming along. If you expect wreaths and festoons, you will be disappointed; if you look for cornucopias, you will not find them; if you have called up a vision of Cupid swinging on a rope of roses over the doorway, you will not realize that vision. You find simply a plain brick house, bearing no other emblem of the trade carried on within than a pair of iron extinguishers on each side of the doorway, in which, by a considerable stretch of the imagination, you may conceive the torch of Hymen to have been occasionally quenched, at a period prior to the introduction of gas. Neither the red rose, nor the blue violet, nor the sweet carnation, embowers the windows; these being wholly unadorned, rather dingy, and provided each with a wire blind, on which are painted, in the severest prose, the words "Cupid and Co., Manufacturers."

Entering that mundane doorway, and wiping my feet on that cocoa-nut mat, of the earth earthy, I could not conceive the realm of sublimated fancy which lay beyond. With a lively impression of what was afterwards revealed to me, I feel now that it was like going up the greasy gallery-stairs of a theatre, to find the transformation scene on, and all the fairies gracefully reposing in the Bower of Bliss.

I was not, however, inducted to the mysteries too suddenly. A youth, in all the elegance of turned-up shirt-sleeves, came and took my card, and I had to wait in the counting-house—Cupid's counting-house!—until he returned, which he eventually did, quite at his leisure, whistling what at first hearing appeared to be Love's Young Dream, but which I presently recognized as a melody less in harmony with the genius loci—namely, The Whole Hog or None. Would I step this way? I did so with a nervous hesitation natural to the novelty of my position, and next moment found myself confronted with a remarkably good-looking little gentleman, who acknowledged, in answer to my polite insinuation in that direction, that he was Cupid.

I don't know that I was quite prepared for

the personal appearance he presented. It had never occurred to me to picture the God of Love, even in his manufacturing capacity, otherwise than in a full suit of wings and with a bow and arrow. But here he stood before me in a black frock-coat and a pair of—possibly Sydenham—trousers. A little reflection, however, reconciled me to the make up. I had thought of Cupid as he appears on high days and holidays. But here he was "in business." No doubt the wings were carefully doubled down under the broadcloth, and the bow and arrow were propably hung up in the best bed-room with the pink fleshings, ready for Sunday. Cupid received me with a courtesy which was most flattering, considering that I had come there, a stranger, boldly preferring a request to be shown over his establishment, and initiated into the mysteries of his craft. He was ready to show me all without reserve, and, leading the way, he introduced me at once into the press-room.

It was like a chamber in the mint. The knobbed arms of five or six fly-presses were swinging about so near each other that it seemed impossible to steer through them without being dashed to pieces. I did not try. The presses were stopped, and I was shown how a plain sheet of paper was prepared for a lace-edged valentine.

Every one is familiar with the process of die-stamping, so this part of the operation will not require minute description. The paper is laid upon the matrice, the arms of the press are swung round and the die descends, embossing the paper by one pressure. But the dies here are no ordinary dies, and the process is yet far from complete. Each die consists of a heavy square block of iron enclosed with the matrice in a metal box, which is furnished with two handles like the legs of a pair of tongs, for the convenience of the operator. The design, after being drawn upon the surface of the iron, is hammered into it by means of steel punches. The iron of the die, of course, is softer—or rather I should say less hard—than the material of the punch; but when the design is completed the die is hardened by the usual process of tempering. A great number and variety of punches are required to execute a design. For example, in an embossed border every little hexagon, every dot, and every flower requires a separate punch.

The execution of a design, therefore, is a tedious and expensive process. There are, perhaps, a hundred different dies about the room, and some of them have cost nearly twenty pounds. The matrices are made of mill-board, and, ranged on shelves on the walls, look like a library of well-thumbed, dog-eared books. I am now standing aside, and the fly-presses are in full swing embossing two or three sheets of paper each per minute. Some of these sheets are plain; others contain a picture in the centre, as, for example, the before-mentioned lady and gentleman, who, with the pathway and the church, have already been printed on the paper by the familiar process of lithography. They are now receiving embossed borders.

The next process is to convert these borders into paper lace, with all the interstices proper to the particular kind which the design represents. The dies are removed from the presses, and with the embossed sheets handed over to a distinct set of workmen in another room. These workmen, who practise this branch of the manufacture solely and exclusively, lay the embossed paper neatly on the die, adjusting it exactly by means of regulating pins at the corners, and then with flat iron tools covered with fine sand-paper, rub off the projecting bosses on the paper. This process is very neatly and rapidly performed, and a strip of Valenciennes or Mechlin starts up under the tool at every rub.

In this room a dozen workmen do nothing else all day long but use the sand-paper file. It is a very magical way of making lace, and the operation seems easy, bnt it is not so easy as it seems. It requires great nicety of touch not to tear the paper. One of the pressmen down-stairs, who essayed to complete the process for my benefit, signally failed with the sand-paper file, and tore what might have been a gorgeous messenger of love, all to tatters.

Let us follow our valentine step by step from its cradle to—I will not say its grave, but to that neat white box in which it is packed, with others of its kind, to be sent out to the trade. Let us say that we begin with the sheet of paper bearing the plain, unadorned presentment of the lady and gentleman lovingly wending their way towards the sacred fane. We have seen them encompassed by an embossed border; we have seen that border magically transformed into lace. But still, with all this, the valentine remains in the penny plain condition. Now, however, it passes into the twopence coloured department—a long room, containing some twenty neat-handed nymphs seated at a bench, each with a little pot of liquid water-colour at her elbow.

Valentine comes into the hand of nymph number one. Nymph lies it flat before her, and places over its surface a perforated sheet of cardboard, the perforations in which correspond exactly with, say the pathway. The brush is dipped in the pot of pale brown and daubed over the perforations. Behold the pale brown pathway! The valentine passes to nymph number two, who uses another stencil plate of cardboard, and daubs in the salmon-coloured church. Number three in the same manner dashes in the gentleman's blue coat, number four his yellow waistcoat, number five his lilac continuations, number six the lady's green mantle, number seven the lady's pink bonnet, while it probably remains for other nymphs to clothe the fields with verdure, and indicate the smiling morn by tipping the hills with gold.

Thus a highly-coloured valentine passes through at least half a dozen hands in the process of colouring, or pooning, as it is technically called. The pooning cards, perforated with all sorts of irregular holes, and daubed with various colours, have a very odd appearance, lying together in a heap on a bench. A stranger to these mysteries could not possibly guess the use of such queer things. He would probably arrive at the conclusion that they were the efforts, not of methodical genius, but of most unmethodical madness.

When our valentine has passed through this room, it is, for all ordinary purposes, complete, and, with a lace border and highly-coloured illustration, may be sold at prices varying from sixpence to half-a-crown; but if it aspire to value itself at five shillings or half a guinea, it must yield to further adornment in another department.

Again, a long room occupied by nymphs, each one having at her elbow a pot, not of colour this time, but of glue. Strewed before each girl in apparent confusion, but really in regularly-assorted heaps, lie hearts and darts and doves and bows and arrows, and rosebuds and true lovers' knots, and torches of Hymen, and every variety of emblem appertaining to love and matrimony. These ornaments are cut out of every kind of material by means of punches. Some are paper, some are silk and velvet, some tinsel and gold-leaf. The business of the girls here is to stick these ornaments upon the valentines, so as perhaps to enclose the picture in a posie of flowers and emblems.

Our lady and gentleman are now under treatment. You will observe that there is an unadorned space between the border and the picture. This is about to be filled up, and the basis of the operation is a series of paper springs. Cupid, who is in close attendance, explaining everything in the most obliging manner, says to the nymph, "Show the gentleman how you make paper springs." It is done in a moment. A strip of writing-paper is doubled lengthways alternately backwards and forwards three times—in the form of a pipe-light—and then cut into lengths of about half an inch.

The lower ends of these springs are fastened to the valentine with glue, and then upon the upper surfaces are fixed strips of plain flat paper. Upon these strips the nymph, according to a design which lies before her, arranges flowers and love-knots and all kinds of devices. Immediately over the church she glues on a gilt Cupid; at the corners she places birds'-nests with eggs; down the side, festoons of flowers, relieved here and there with united hearts and crossed darts and lyres and flying doves.

This decoration forms a pretty bas-relief frame to the picture, and the paper springs which support it permit the frame to be pressed flat for the convenience of packing. Each of the girls in this department is at work upon a different design, some of which are exceedingly pretty and tasteful. Some, too, are very expensive. Here, for example, is one containing in the centre a really well-executed picture, in the ivory miniature style, of Cupid, surrounded by a rich ornamental border studded with pearls.

The price of this elegant article, enclosed in an enamelled box neatly tied up with white satin ribbon, is two guineas. I am naturally curious to know if many of these are sold. The answer to my query is, "A good many." I am informed, however, that the most expensive chiefly go to the colonies. I could imagine a gold-digger buying this valentine with the pearls and paying for it with a nugget. It seems very absurd to give two guineas for a valentine, but the one under notice really appears to be worth the money. It is a most elaborate affair, and, as a piece of delicate workman and workwomanship, *looks* to be better worth the price than many fancy articles of more intrinsic value which we see in the windows of the jewellers. The brightly-coloured varnished flowers that are used in this department have hitherto been made almost exclusively in Germany, but Cupid informs me, with great satisfaction, that he will shortly be in a position to compete with the Germans on their own ground, and dispense with foreign aid altogether.

Our lady and gentleman are now proceeding to church under every imaginable circumstance of glory. Cupid keeps watch over them with more than a cherub's personality, doves flutter round them, flowers bloom at their feet, while the air is laden with a rich perfume, emanating, I am bound to state, from a pinch of Jockey Club artfully inserted in a piece of cotton wool, and stowed away under the exalted seat of Cupid.

Still our lady and gentleman have to pass through another ordeal. They must step into the next room and be examined. Nymphs again are the examiners, and there are six of them. They sit here permanently, as a committee of taste. If there be anything wrong, a dove flying with its feet in the air, a Cupid standing on his head, or a rose violating the laws of nature by growing downward, the lady and gentleman are sent back to have their glorious surroundings put to rights; if not, they receive the imprimatur of approval, and are placed in cardboard boxes to be delivered to the trade.

In following the progress of our valentine from the embossing-room to the finishing department, we have passed in review about sixty hands, nearly forty of these being girls, the rest men and boys. In all the departments the work struck me as being of a healthy and cheerful kind. The rooms are well lighted and airy, and the girls exhibit none of the languor and weariness which are painfully apparent in the work-rooms of the milliner and dressmaker. They are very neatly dressed, and some of them are very pretty, and these appearences, together with a briskness of manner and a cheerfulness of expression, convinced me that if the Song of the Valentine were written, it would form a happy contrast to the Song of the Shirt.

The girls work from eight o'clock in the morning till seven o'clock at night, with intervals for dinner and tea, and their wages range from five to fifteen shillings a week, the average being ten for the skilled hands, and five for young beginners—mere children, who certainly could not earn as much money at anything else.

Although there are slack and busy seasons in this trade, as in every other, the employment is pretty regular all the year round. At this moment artists and die-sinkers are at work for next year. About June or July their designs will be finished, and copies struck off for the travellers who go out with their pattern-books, as early as August. And there are articles besides valentines made here; articles which come in at unpoetical seasons, to keep the machinery of the establishment in full play.

Among those lace dies in the press-room, you will find a considerable number of dies for printing trade marks—labels for bottles, and tinsel devices for linen and calico, duly registered—to imitate which is now a misdemeanor, punishable with fine and imprisonment. The trade marks for linen and cotton fabrics, however, are quite in the valentine style, and only fall short of ideality only so far as they are minus poetry. Here, for example, is an oval device in silver paper, in the midst of which a lady of the ballet is standing on the very tips of her toes, gracefully surrounding her lovely form by a scarf—the whole being designed to give the stamp of authenticity to a bale of muslin, which is possibly destined to be cut up for bridal garments.

I scarcely expected in Cupid's manufactory to meet with an important and significant commercial fact. But I did. It is, that the demand for trade marks for cotton goods, which fell off suddenly at the beginning of the American war, and which a year ago ceased almost entirely, is now again becoming active. A sign of reviving trade among the symbols of languishing love, which I commend to the notice of the City-article writers. It is also worthy of note, that the export trade in valentines is reviving. That, too, was damaged by the Transatlantic struggle: there being naturally no corner of love in hearts inflamed with anger and hate.

But let not considerations of commerce and politics interfere with the higher claims of art. Two of the questions which I often put to myself in the days when I was wholly ignorant of the great valentine economy yet remain unanswered. Who draws the pictures? Who writes the poetry? For a practical elucidation of this mystery we very properly and fitly go up-stairs to the higher regions of the establishment. In a well-lighted room, exclusively devoted to art, we find six draughtsmen transferring their designs to stone. The designs are highly finished and elaborately coloured, and some of them are really beautiful. They don't look so well when they are printed, for much the same reason that a wood-engraving rarely comes up to the original drawing. They are spoilt by the heavy-handed process of colouring, as the drawing on wood is often marred by the engraver. There are no middle tints. It goes, if you will excuse the popular phrase, the whole hog or none. Bright blue or nothing, blood red and no surrender!

Looking, however, at some of the drawings, I can detect no fault in them. I have seen worse things on the stairs of the Royal Academy. But these designs are intended for the superior order of valentines. The common kinds and the comic kinds are drawn out of doors. Nothing coarse or vulgar is issued from this establishment, and the common specimens are only common, in so far as the paper is inferior and the drawing is dashed in with more regard to effect than finish.

The subjects of some of the comic valentines are copied from drawings in Punch and his humorous contemporaries, but the great majority of them are original, and deal mainly with the passing follies and fashions of the day—crinoline, the Dundreary whiskers, the jacket coat, the spoon bonnet, and so forth. The regular comic artist of the establishment—a very clever fellow, by the way—does not work on the premises: his fancy being probably of too buoyant a nature to brook being chained to a bench, or controlled by regular hours. I understand that he is a highly prosperous person, that he drives up to the door in a Hansom cab, and is very sharp and short with the head of the firm.

The poet, too, works out; but it was my happiness to meet him on the door-step on taking my leave. I am bound to say that he looked like a poet. He had raven ringlets, wore a cloak with a velvet collar, and had a fine phrensy in his eye. I caught it just as it was rolling, and I said to myself, "Nascitur, non fit." What does he sing of our lady and gentleman churchward-bound along the pale brown pathway?

The path before me gladly would I trace,
With one who's dearest to my constant heart,
To yonder church, the holy sacred place,
Where I my vows of Love would fain impart;
And in sweet wedlock's bonds unite with thee,
Oh, then, how blest my life would ever be!

And there is that rather sporting-looking young man, in the green waistcoat and the pink necktie, grasping by the hand the generally blue maiden in the gipsy hat under the cliffs—apparently, of Dover—who thus pours forth his soul:

Ne'er doubt, fair maid, the vows I make,
A constant heart no time can shake;
Rather than cause it e'er to wander,
Time, the true heart, makes grow fonder.

Our poet is evidently of a serious turn, and given to the sentimental and the pathetic; finds it difficult to screw himself down to the low level of the comic. There is quite a touch of the pastoral style in the opening line of his satire upon the lady in the spoon bonnet:

Tell me, gentle lady fair,
Why such ugly things you wear,
Surely all your wits are fled,
A spoon to carry on your head.

He is almost didactic in his severity upon the gentleman with the scrubbing-brush beard, who is admiring himself in the looking-glass:

Looking at thyself within the glass,
You appear lost in admiration;
You deceive yourself, and think, alas!
You are a wonder of creation.

If it be alleged that the poet-laureate of Love is somewhat halt, it must be remembered that Love himself is blind. I have not heard that a butt of sherris sack forms part of the reward of Cupid's laureate; but I believe his verses are estimated as being worth twopence a line, which is, at any rate, a penny over the conventionally standard price of prose. At this price, the poem just quoted would come to eightpence. But the great difficulty in dealing with the valentine poet is to make him comprehend that brevity is not only the soul of wit, but the essence of economy. His efforts are very frequently vain, owing to his strong disposition to spin the subject out so as to make even money of it. There are many pounds of poetry up-stairs that would have been declined with thanks had they not been furnished by contract.

It might be imagined that the hard practical nature of our time had tended in some degree to bring the sending of valentines into contempt, as being a practice beneath the dignity of the age. But this is by no means the case. Cupid informs me that, in the height of his season, he turns out two hundred and fifty pounds' worth of valentines a week, and at these times he pays about a hundred and sixty pounds a week in wages. That his business is yearly on the increase is proved by the annual report of the Postmaster-General, which shows that, while the number of valentines which passed through the London office in 1862 was four hundred and thirty thousand, in 1863 it was upwards of four hundred and fifty thousand. The iron of our age has not entered the national soul so deeply, after all.

MY ACCOUNT WITH HER MAJESTY.

I NEVER laid by a penny till the Post-office Savings-banks came up. Not that I mightn't have done so, for I earned good wages, and after paying all the expenses at home, I had always plenty of loose cash to spend. I was never without money in my pocket; but always at the year's end I had spent all I had received. I knew very well that I might have saved a good bit, without cutting down the weekly allowance to the missus for the house, or stinting myself of any reasonable enjoyment; but I had never begun the thing, and when I thought about doing it, I was at a loss how to go about it.

What I used to do, when I had a little lump of money over and above the expenses, was to put it away in a drawer, and lock it up; and I used to say to myself, "I won't touch that money, but I'll put more to it from time to time, and when it amounts to a hundred, I'll do something with it—put it in the bank, or invest it in a building society, or something of that sort."

But, somehow, the money didn't grow as I expected. You see, I always had the key of that drawer in my pocket, and at any time, if I ran a little short through being rather free with my mates or going upon the spree, I had nothing to do but to go to the drawer and help myself. I hesitated over it sometimes, but never for long; the drawer was so handy, and I used to say to myself,

"If I take a sovereign it won't reduce the money much, and I can put it back again next week." But it generally happened when next week came that it wasn't convenient to put the money back.

And so I went on going to the drawer for sovereigns and half-sovereigns, until the bit of money dwindled down so low that it wasn't worth keeping. It's the same with drink. If you make up your mind that you won't taste a drop for a week, and stick to it, you are all right; but only be persuaded to make a beginning—to take one glass, just one, and you take another and another, and then it's all wrong. It's the same, too, I dare say, with swindling and robbing your master: once make a beginning, and on you go, like rolling down One-Tree-hill on Whit-Monday—the further you go, the faster you go.

Susan used to say to me,

"George, how's the money getting on?"

And she used to say it in a sly, sarcastic sort of

way, meaning that I was spending it, and that it was going very fast. I know it was, but I didn't like to acknowledge it, and always said:

"Oh! it's all right in the drawer, there, what's of it."

"Well, George," she would say, "you put away ten pounds about a month ago, and as Christmas is coming on, it will enable us to buy all we require, and give a little party to our friends."

"Yes," I would say, "but you know, my dear, that I have had to pay So-and-so, and So-and-so;" and then I'd name certain bills, and the subscription to my lodge—for I'm an Odd Fellow—and add it up and subtract it from the ten, and Susan, not being good at figures, would be quite puzzled, and give the sum up in despair. But she found me out more than once.

One day, when I came home to dinner, she says to me,

"George," she says, "you left the key of the drawer on the mantelshelf this morning."

She didn't look at me, but went on carving the boiled rabbit. My wife is odd that way, and not like the generality of women. Nagging is not one of her faults. She doesn't say much, but she thinks the more. So when she told me about the key in that quiet way, I knew she had been to the drawer and counted the money. That's where I don't hold with Bluebeard. He might have tried his wife with anything but a secret; it is downright unreasonable to expect a woman not to be curious. I merely said

"Oh!" in an indifferent kind of a way; but I am sure my looks convicted me.

However, Susan did not make any remark about the money being nearly all gone, but, by-and-by, when she was helping me to a suety dumpling she says in her usual demure way,

"Don't you think, George, it would be a good thing to put a little money away in the savings-bank?"

"Well," I says, "it wouldn't be a bad thing, Susan?"

"No," she says, "I'm sure it wouldn't, and if I was you I would make a beginning."

"Well," I says, "I would, if I knew how to go about it."

"There's no difficulty about that," Susan says; "you've only to go to Welbeck-street, and put a little in, and they'll give you a book, and there you are."

"Very well, Susan," I says, "I'll take your advice, and go to Welbeck-street to-morrow."

I was as good as my word, and next day, at the dinner-hour, I walked up to Welbeck-street to put in three pound ten, which was all that was left of the fifteen. But, lo and behold! when I got to the bank it was shut, and for the moment I thought it had broke, or the manager bolted with the funds, or something; but on looking about I noticed a brass-plate on the wall with information about the bank hours, and from that I learned that the bank was only open three days a week, from ten to two in the morning, and from six to eight in the evening. I had come on the wrong day.

I was a good bit vexed to have all my trouble for my pains, but Susan, when I told her, took it quite quiet, and says,

"Never mind, George, you can go again on Saturday, when the bank is open."

Well, I fully resolved to go, and on Saturday morning I took the money with me, intending to walk over to the bank after my work. However, just as I was leaving the shop at six o'clock, who should I meet but an old mate of mine, that I hadn't seen for years. Nothing would do for Dave but I must go and have a glass with him. Well, you know, you can't refuse to drink with a mate, especially when he's been away in Birmingham for ever so long, and got a holiday on purpose to come up and see his friends. So in we goes to the Yorkshire Grey, and has a glass of rum-and-water each, and you know how the time slips away when old friends meet as have been long parted. Dave had so much to tell me about Birmingham gun-barrels, and I had so much to tell Dave about Clerkenwell watch-springs, and one thing followed another, including glasses of rum-and-water, that it was a quarter to eight in no time. It was no use; I couldn't get to Welbeck-street in a quarter of an hour unless I took a cab, and it didn't seem natural like to take a cab to go to a savings-bank with three pound ten: so I stopped with Dave and had another glass.

When I went home and told Susan, she didn't say an angry word, but just remarked that I was very unlucky. You don't know how aggravating Susan is in that way. I'd rather have tongue-pie a good deal, than that sit-and-say-nothing, but think-the-more way of hers. It's more. aggravating than saying the thing right out; for you can't tell what an awful character a quiet woman *thinks* you are. For my part, I'd rather have tea-cups. However, I was resolved to show Susan that I was in earnest, and on the following Tuesday I got to the bank in good time.

I didn't find it such an easy matter, though, to put my money away, even now when I was there with it in my hand. There was such a lot of people in the bank that there was no getting near the counter for full a quarter of an hour, and when at last I did get to it, the clerks didn't seem inclined to take any notice of me. Two or three times I said to one of them that I wanted to put in three pound ten, but he paid no attention, and always turned to somebody else. An old woman with half-a-crown cut me out first, and then I was elbowed aside by a charity-boy with a shilling all in coppers. They were regular customers, and used to the banking business, I suppose, and I wasn't. However, I got it in at last, and received my book, and I do assure you I felt a load taken off my mind.

When I showed the book to Susan, she said,

"That's right, George, and I hope you'll go on with it."

I fully intended to do so then; but it's easy to intend, and not so easy to carry your intendings out. It's like sitting over a fire on a winter's night, and saying, "I'll get up early to-morrow morning and do over-time;" but when the morning comes, and you peep out between the clothes and see the frost upon the windows, it's very easy to find an excuse for lying a little longer.

The evening song and the morning song don't often agree. So it was with my saving. I had always a pretty lively recollection of the trouble it was to walk all the way to Welbeck-street after my day's work, and then to have to push my way through a crowd of old women, and wait my turn at the counter. It's not worth doing for a few shillings, I used to say to myself; I'll wait until there's more of it, and then put in a lump. So I put the shillings away in the drawer until such time as they should grow to be pounds; but owing to the key being always handy they didn't, and what with club-nights and sprees now and then, it never came to be enough to be worth while taking down to Welbeck-street.

When Christmas-time came, all I had in the bank was the three pounds ten I first put in. However, that was something, and as I was rather short just then, it would come in handy to get the Christmas extras. Three days before Christmas I went down to the bank to draw the money out, promising Susan to come straight home with it. You may judge how mad I was, when the clerk told me that I couldn't draw the money out without giving a week's notice. Here was a pretty go; Susan at home waiting for the money to get in the tea and sugar, the plums and currants, and what not, and the cash not be got until after Christmas.

"This sort of saving won't suit me," says I to myself; "there's too much ceremony about it."

I had to borrow the money from one of my mates to get my Christmas dinner, and at the end of the week I drew my money out of Welbeck-street, and paid him back; and that was the end of my account at that savings-bank.

Next year Susan belonged to a pudding club at the grocer's, and I belonged to a goose club at the Yorkshire Grey. We began to pay in sixpence a week very shortly after Midsummer, and a few days before Christmas, Susan brought home a parcel of groceries, and I got a goose, and a bottle of gin, and a bottle of rum. We didn't miss the money paid every week in sixpences, and when the things came home, they seemed like a gift. I said to Susan that I thought this was better than putting money in the savings-bank, where there was so much ceremony, and Susan thought so too. But when Susan's brother, John, who is a cashier at a large linendraper's, came to dinner on Christmas-day, and we told him how we had been saving, he burst out a-laughing.

"What are you laughing at?" I says.

"What am I laughing at?" he says, almost choking himself with a mouthful of goose—"why, at you."

"What for?" I says.

"For being so jolly green," he says.

"Jolly green!" I says; "is it jolly green to lay by money for a rainy day?—leastways, for Christmas-day, when a family requires extras?"

"Fiddlesticks!" John says: "Let me ask you a question, George."

"Twenty," I says; "go ahead, John."

"Well," he says, "when did you begin to pay into the goose-club at the Yorkshire Grey?"

"At Midsummer," I says.

"And you paid in sixpence every week for twenty-six weeks?"

"Yes," I says, "I did."

"Which made thirteen shillings, George?"

"Exactly," I says.

"Well," he says, "is the goose and liquor worth it?"

"Judge for yourself, John," I says. "Could I have bought such a goose as that you are now partaking of for less than eight-and-six in the shops?"

"No," he says, "I don't think you could."

"Very well," I says, "where's your fiddlesticks, and how do you make me out jolly green?"

"Why, this way, George," he says: "in the first place, you've been losing the interest upon your money for six months."

"That's not much," I says.

"No," he says, "perhaps not; but that's not

all. I'll be bound to say, George, if you'll only be candid enough to confess it, that every time you went to the Yorkshire Grey to pay in sixpence to the goose-club, you had a glass of something?"

"I don't deny it," I says; "you can't well go to a public-house without having a glass."

"Sometimes two," he says.

"Well," I says, "sometimes two; perhaps three, when I happened to meet a friend."

"Then, let us say, George, that every time you went to pay in sixpence to the club, you spent, on an average, another sixpence on drink."

"It might be about that," I says.

"Very well then, George, upon your own showing, your goose, and bottle of gin, and bottle of rum, have cost you six-and-twenty shillings, to say nothing of your loss of time, and the injury to your constitution through drinking more than was good for you."

"I never thought of it in that way, John," I says.

"No, of course not, George," he says; "for if you had thought of it in that way you wouldn't have been such a fool as to do it."

"But you'll admit," I says, "that Susan has had her money's-worth at the grocer's, and not paid more than she ought."

"I am not going to dispute that," he says; "but you must remember the grocer has had the use of her money, and supposing he had failed about the beginning of December, what would have become of Susan, and all the other Christmas-club geese? I'm surprised at a sensible man like you, George, doing such things, when there's a Post-office Savings-bank close to your door."

"But," I says, "there's so much ceremony about savings-banks; they're only open certain days a week, and the hours are inconvenient for a working man, and——"

"You don't know anything about them, George," he says, taking me up short; for the Post-office Savings-banks that have just come up are open every day from ten to four, and you may put money in, and draw it out, whenever you like."

"Well, John," I says. "I'll see about it."

I did see about it, and found that one of the Post-office banks had been opened at Bardsley's, the tea-grocer's, in the next street. Bardsley's is our post-office and money-order office as well; and walking up the shop through an avenue of sugar-loaves, I found a clerk reading the newspaper.

"I want to put some money in the new bank," I says.

The clerk never said a word, but placed a printed paper before me to sign. I read it over and signed it, thereby declaring that I was not directly or indirectly entitled to any deposit in that, or any other savings-bank, and that I submitted myself to the rules of the Post-office Savings-bank. The clerk then handed me a small paper book, about the size of a penny memorandum book, only it had a white cover with the royal arms at the top, and was printed all over with rules and regulations.

"Sign your name on that line, across the inside of the cover," the clerk says.

I signed it.

"That's your signature," he says, "for drawing out, and you should be particular always to use the same one."

I then handed the clerk five shillings as my first deposit. He took the money, wrote in the book, "Number 857. 1862. Jan. 1. — — 5," put the post-office letter stamp for the day against the entry, and the thing was done. I don't think I was more than five minutes in the shop altogether. The very next evening, when Susan and I were sitting at supper, the postman came to the door. Susan answered him, and came back with a letter in her hand.

"Lor', George," she says, "it's a letter, 'On

Her Majesty's Service;' whatever can it be about? I shouldn't wonder if it was the water-rates, for you know the man has called three times, and—"

"There, let's open it," I says, "that's the best way to find out what it's about. It's all right, Susan," I says; "it's a letter from the Postmaster-General."

"And whatever does *he* want?" Susan says.

"Oh, nothing," I says; "he only writes to say that five shillings have been placed to my credit in the books of his department."

"Well, it's very condescending of him," Susan says, "for so little."

"Well," I says, "it's a guarantee that it's all right, and there's his signature, 'Geo. Chetwynd.'"

"Cheatwind!" Susan says; "are you sure it's all safe, George?"

"Safe as the bank," I says, "and safer; for the Queen, the two Houses of Parliament, and all the taxes, are security."

I quite took a fancy to the Post-office Savings-bank when I found how simple the machinery was. It was almost as handy as the drawer, to have a bank round the corner where you could buy your tea and sugar, and put your money away all at once, and without ceremony. I was as pleased with it as a child with a pretty toy, and I liked the importance of receiving letters every now and then "On Her Majesty's Service." Susan used to put the letters on the chimney-piece for people to see. It was soon the talk of the neighbourhood that I was holding a correspondence with the government, and it was reported that I was going to be appointed watchmaker to the Queen and the royal family. I passed the post-office twice every day on coming home to dinner and going back again to work, and to walk in with my book and put away a few shillings, was just like dropping in to the public-house to have a glass of ale. And always the next day, whether it was pounds or shillings, I had a letter "On Her Majesty's Service;" and Susan would meet me at the door and say,

"George, here's another letter from the Queen."

And then we'd sit down after supper and count it up, and see how much I had at my banker's. I found putting money away in the Post-office Savings-bank so easy and so pleasant like, that I rather overdid the thing, and put more money away than I could spare. So one day I ran short, and had to draw out. It was almost as easy and expeditious as drawing a cheque upon one of the big banks. At the post-office they gave me a slip of paper with a form of withdrawal upon it, and addressed in print to the Postmaster-

General on the back. I had nothing to do but fill in the number of my book, the amount I wanted to draw out, sign my name, double the bit of paper up, and shove it in the post. It only took me about a minute, for the paper was ready gummed for sealing, and no stamp was required, it being marked on the back, "On Her Majesty's Service." It was two o'clock on Tuesday when I posted the letter. At four o'clock next day I had an answer in the shape of a printed form, very similar to the notice paper. I had nothing to do but sign it and present it at the post-office, and the money was handed to me, the clerk marking off the withdrawal in my book.

It's my belief that saving is a habit, like smoking, or taking snuff, or like extravagance. If you begin it and go on with it for a little time, you come to have a sort of passion for it. Whenever I had any spare cash, I was off to Bardsley's with it, and often when I thought of withdrawing some I didn't do it, saying to myself,

"Oh, I can give notice to-morrow, or the next day, or any time I like;" and so perhaps I waited and tided over the temporary difficulty, and didn't withdraw at all.

About the beginning of December, in 'sixty-three, when I went to put in three pounds, the clerk wouldn't take it.

"What's up," I says," going to stop?"

"No," he says; "but if you look at the rules and regulations in your book, you'll find that you ain't allowed to put in more than thirty pounds a year."

That, I believe, is to protect the regular bankers, and it may be quite right, but I don't exactly see it. I know this, that before the new year, when I might begin to put in again, I had blewed that three pound which the clerk wouldn't take. If it did any good to the regular bankers, it certainly didn't do any good to me. However, at the end of 'sixty-three, I had fifty pounds at the Post-office Savings-bank, and I might have had sixty, only I took a holiday in August, and went down with Susan for a week to Margate, where we were rather free. And here I found out another advantage of this wonderful Post-office bank. Susan and I went boating, and raffling, and driving in chaises, and ran short, and were likely to be in a fix, until I looked over the rules and regulations in my bank-book, when I learned that I might withdraw my money at any Post-office Savings-bank in the kingdom, by giving notice to that effect. So I sent up the usual notice of withdrawal to London — I keep a dozen of them stitched together in a cover, and call it my cheque-book—stating that I wanted to withdraw the money at the post-office at Margate; and, almost by return, back came the withdrawal paper, and I had nothing to do but go to the post-office and get it cashed. And the forms don't cost you a farthing; there's no postage to pay, and when the time comes for you to send up your book to the chief office in London for the interest at two and a half per cent. to be calculated and added to your account—which is the anniversary of the day on which the first deposit was made—the Postmaster-General sends you a big envelope for the purpose.

Altogether, it's the best-regulated thing I ever came across, and if it doesn't make people save, nothing will. But it does, I'm sure. Look at Bardsley's shop now, to what it was. Why, that little box with the pigeon-hole, where they used to do the post-office order business, has swollen into a great banking department, and there's Bardsley himself, with a clerk to help him, at it all day long, with piles of bank-notes and bowls full of sovereigns beside them—just like Twining's or the Bank of England itself. Bardsley's proud of it too; I know he is. He's never behind the counter now, serving tea and sugar; he leaves that to his young men; he's a banker, bless you.

I don't believe I should ever have saved anything if these Post-office Savings-banks hadn't come up; and I'm sure if it was generally known how handy and convenient they are, thousands like myself would take advantage of them, and soon learn to be careful and provident. If there's a philanthropist that's hard up for an object, I don't know what he could do better than go about distributing tracts setting forth the rules and regulations and advantages of the Post-office Savings-banks.

EXCEEDINGLY ODD FELLOWS.

George has told you about his account at the Post-office Savings-bank, and would have you believe that he was a model of prudence, and all that sort of thing.* But I could tell you a different story. Not that I mind what he says about me being aggravating, and sitting and saying nothing, and that being worse than nagging, for I despise such insinuations; but George, though he is my husband, and as kind and good a man as ever breathed, is a fool with his money, and that's the truth. His putting money in the Post-office Savings-bank is just a fad, and I feel certain that if I don't look after him, he will make ducks and drakes of it after all. He told you that he is an Odd Fellow. Well do I know it. The state that he comes home in after the lodge meetings, which are held at that horrid Yorkshire Grey, is dreadful. To hear him coming up to bed at two o'clock in the morning, you would think they was shooting coals up the stairs. And then when he comes into the bedroom, trying to walk straight and holding on by

* See My Account with Her Majesty.

the chest of drawers, and I give him a look, he says,

"Don't look like that, Susan; you know I have been at the lodge providing for a rainy day, and doing my duty to my family."

I must say this of George, that always when he's been providing for a rainy day and doing his duty to his family, he comes home smelling of rum with lemon.

When George first joined the Odd Fellows I thought it was a very good thing, for he told me, that by paying in a small sum every month, he would get ten shillings a week if he ever happened to be laid up, and ten pounds for burial expenses if he died, which of course would be a nice thing to have, and one-and-ninepence a month not too much to pay for it. But after a bit there were so many lodge meetings, and George so often coming home tight, that I began to think one-and-ninepence couldn't do it, so I was determined to get to the bottom of it, and one day I catechised him.

"Whatever do you do at that lodge, George?" I says.

"Do," he says, "why, transact business, of course."

"But it surely doesn't take you till two o'clock in the morning," I says.

"Oh yes it does," he says; "the business is sometimes very heavy, and there's a great many accounts to go through, and the affairs of the order to discuss, and lots of things—lor' bless you, you have no idea what a great society ours is; it's bigger than the Freemasons': we have hundreds of thousands of members all over the country, and more than a million of money, and an Act of Parliament all to our own selves."

Well, of course, when he told me that they had so much money, and an Act of Parliament all to themselves, I thought it must be all right. But, by-and-by, there was a deal too much of the lodge to please me. Whenever I wanted him to come home early, or to take me to the theatre, it was always,

"I can't to-night, Susan, for I've to go to the lodge."

"But it ain't the lodge night, George," I used to say.

"No," he would answer, "but there's a special meeting to-night, and I must not miss it, as I expect soon to be G. M."

"Why, what's that?" I says.

"Oh," he says, "Grand Master, Susan, which is the highest office there is in our society, and an honour to them as is elected to it."

"Well," I says, "George, it may be a very

fine thing for you to be G. M., but it ain't pleasant for me sitting here moping at home night after night till one, two, three, and four in the morning, and you always coming home smelling as you do of rum, which doesn't look to me like business."

I was determined to know what they did at the lodge; and so one night, when I thought George and the members would be in the midst of their business, I put on my bonnet and shawl and a thick dotted veil, walked down to the Yorkshire Grey, and slipped into the parlour, which I knew was next to the large room where the Odd Fellows held their meetings. I had a glass of shrub and a biscuit, and told the young man that, as I was rather tired, I would sit and rest myself a bit. Well, I hadn't been there five minutes before I heard voices in the next room, and George's above all, crying, "Order, order!"

And then I heard somebody say,

"Oh, bother the accounts; put them books away, and let's get to business."

"Hear, hear!" everybody cried, and there was a tremendous knocking on the tables, and a voice called out,

"Give your orders, gentlemen, the waiter is in the room;" and then there was a scuffling about and a chinking of glasses, and after a little delay, a voice cried out,

"Tile the door, Joseph, Brother Bensley will oblige."

I heard a bolt go, there was more knocking on the tables, and then somebody—Brother Bensley, I suppose—began to sing the "Haymakers" through his nose, and after each verse they all took up the chorus.

At the end of this song, which seemed to be applauded with hammers, I heard another voice ask,

"What shall we say after that, Brother Bensley?" and Brother Bensley replied,

"May the present moment be the worst of our lives." Everybody cried "Hear, hear, hear!" and the hammer went at it again. I stopped a full hour, and this sort of thing went on all the time. After each song, it was always,

"Give your orders, gentlemen, the waiter is in the room;" and then,

"Tile the door, Joseph, Brother this, that, or the other will oblige."

Then the bolt went, and the song began, and the company took up the chorus and clapped their hands and knocked, and made such a noise as I never heard.

Well, I couldn't with conscience remain any

longer on a glass of shrub and a biscuit, so I went away and took a walk as far as John's, and stopped with Jane for more than an hour, and went back again to the Yorkshire Grey about eleven; and would you believe it, they were still at it, singing choruses and hammering on the tables like mad. And I hadn't listened outside for more than five minutes, before I heard my George singing Home sweet Home, and I knew very well by his voice what state he was in.

Some women would have walked right into the room and had him out there and then; but whatever my feelings may be, a thing I never will do is to go and fetch my husband out of the public-house. If a man demeans himself in such a place, that's no reason a woman should; and from all I hear you don't get anything by it but dirt thrown in your face, as the publican always sides with his customers, and a wife as goes and interferes with her husband, when he is spending his money and enjoying himself, is looked upon as a curse.

So I didn't wait to see or hear any more, but went straight home, and, the fire not being out, sat up for George, determined to give him a bit of my mind for once. It was past one when he arrived. I knew what state he was in before he came in, by the way he boggled with the latch-key, which is a thing I am sorry I ever consented to, and which I might have nipped in the bud if I had begun in time; but let such things only take root, and grow, and it's a charter ever afterwards. You wouldn't believe the artfulness of George when he's half-seas over.

I often wonder how he can do it, with the drink in and the wit out as it is, when he comes home in that state? He'll stand just for a minute in the passage to balance himself, and then he'll come in with a bounce to make believe that he's brisk, and steady, and all right. And always when he comes in like that he smiles—oh, so idiotic!—and says, "Well."

And I says, "Is it well?" and gives him a look which he can't abear, I know.

"Don't be angry, Susan?" he says; "I didn't intend to stop out so late, but the business of the lodge was rather heavy to-night, and——"

"Fiddlesticks!" I says.

"Oh, don't talk like that, Susan," he says; "you know it's for my good and yours too."

"What!" I says, "drinking, and smoking, and singing songs to this hour in the morning! it's for the good of the Yorkshire Grey—that's whose good it's for. I know what your business is—it's hip, hip, hurrah, bravo, a very good song, and very well sung; give your orders, gentlemen, the waiter's in the room; tile the door, Joseph,

Brother George will oblige with Home sweet Home. Oh, you like your sweet home better than the Yorkshire Grey, don't you?"

"Susan," he says, "I can't stand this."

"No," I says, "you can't abear to be told of your faults; but you shan't complain that I'm aggravating because I sit and say nothing; I intend to speak my mind, now, and I tell you, George, you are a great big pigeon that flies down every other night to the Yorkshire Grey to be plucked. Odd Fellows, indeed. Old fools you are, the lot of you."

You should have seen how George opened his eyes to hear me come out like that. He flopped down in a chair, and sat staring at me like a stuck pig, and all he said was "La, Susan."

"You know now what I think of you, George," I says, "and let me tell you that I know all about your Odd Fellows' Society, and your lodge nights, and your courts, and your benefits, and all the rest of the rubbish."

"Rubbish!" he says.

"Rubbish," I says; "what's all this but rubbish?" and I out with the drawer, and flung all his regalia, as he calls them, in a heap before him on the floor.

"What do you call this?" I says, and I took them up one by one—a blue sash embroidered with the arms of the order, a ridiculous thing for all the world like the picture in Zadkiel's almanack, a satin apron, a silk velvet collar, a gold sash tie, a silver star, a gold tassel, and two rosettes.

"One would think," I says, "that you was a sweep, and that you had got all these rags together to go out with Jack-in-the-Green on the first of May. And here's the bill," I says; "sash with the ridiculous arms of the order, eight-and-six; apron six shillings, collar five shillings, sash-tie one-and-nine, star one-and-six, tassel one-and-nine, rosettes three-and-six—total, one pound nine shillings, and all to make a guy of yourself."

"Well, but you know, Susan," he says, "these things are necessary to distinguish the order and keep it together."

"And a pretty thing to keep together," I says, "if all be true."

"All be true," he says, "what do you mean?"

"I mean," I says, "what's written in this book, which my brother John gave me last night, and told me to be sure and read it to you."

"What book is it?" he says.

"It's what they call a blue-book," I says.

"La, Susan," he says, "who would have thought of you reading a blue-book?"

"I shouldn't have thought it myself," I says,

"for I always thought as they were dry things as nobody ever did read, but used to wrap up butter and light the fire with; but I find different," I says, "for this blue-book, which is by Mr Tidd Pratt, a gentleman under government, tells a many things which is only right that every working man's wife should know.

"If you are able to keep your eyes open," I says, "just listen to this, which is the evidence of a working man like yourself, who was fool enough to go and be an Odd Fellow: 'It has been the custom among the members ever since the commencement of this society, which was in 1837, to spend in drink every club night at the rate of threepence from every member, which was taken out of the contributions, and which will amount up to the present time to £367 4s. Every member was compelled to pay one shilling for drink on the feast day, whether he came or not, besides eight shillings a year spent for drink on committee nights, and for the last seventeen years it exceeds nine shillings a year, and sixpence extra paid for every person becoming a member on club nights, and one shilling extra on becoming a member on feast days.' And here's the bill all regularly made out. Spent in drink, from 9th September, 1837, to 15th October, 1862:

	£	s.	d.
On club nights	367	4	0
On feast nights . .	176	15	0
On committee nights . .	10	17	0
Extra paid by members .	13	4	0
	£ 568	0	0

And all this, besides what the members spent on their own account, for the benefit of the public-house where the lodge was held.

"Another working man tells us that his lodge paid eighteen pounds for a flag and ten pounds for a drum. Now, what on earth a sick fund wants with a drum, is past my comprehension. And perhaps you will just listen to what this poor man says:

"'They have turned me out,' he says, 'because I would not pay for the dinner I never had. They are in the habit, every feast day, of taking so much money out of the box towards drinking—generally about thirty shillings, I think—also sixpence each towards the dinner. There are one or two teetotallers in the club, so last feast day (this I know for a fact) they had taken some money out of the box for drink; one of these teetotallers asked for a glass of teetotal drink; he was refused, and told that he might buy it for himself. Some of the other members stopped till two or three o'clock the next morning to finish the drink bought with the money taken out of the box. Three or four of them were found next morning in a beastly state of intoxication, and carried home.'

"And that's the way you Odd Fellows provide for a rainy day, and do your duty to your families. And here's a nice bill to be charged to the funds of a benevolent society supported by poor working men:

	£	s.	d.
Liquor at monthly meeting	9	0	0
Band at anniversary	6	0	0
Dinners to persons carrying banners	0	6	9
Donation to Lancashire Relief Fund . .	5	0	0
Grant for procession to dinner on the marriage of H.R.H. the Prince of Wales . . .	10	0	0

"Why," I says, "it's nothing but liquor and foolery from beginning to end; ale, grog, dinners, banners, drums, flags, processions, and getting drunk, and all at the expense of the fund that ought to go for sickness and funerals. If you could all be buried in drums," I says, "you might have them with silk flags painted on both sides with the arms of the order for winding sheets, but as for coffins, I don't know where they are to come from."

I declare, if George wasn't a nodding, and fast asleep as a church.

"George," I says, "you have had your evening, and now I'll have mine;" and I stirred him up and made him listen. "Look here," I says, "what Mr Tidd Pratt says, a gentleman as is under government, and his business to know all about. 'The older you get,' he says, 'the worse you get; and in one year,' he says, 'no less than one hundred and thirty-seven friendly societies have been dissolved and wound up,' through not being able to carry on, their expenses being greater than they could afford, all along of ale, and dinners, and drums, and such-like things as are contrary to the Act of Parliament, which you have all to yourselves, and which you are so proud of.

"You brag about your Act of Parliament, but do you know what it says?"

"No," he says, "I never read it, and I suppose nobody ever did."

"Oh yes," I says, "I have, and I can tell you that ale, and feasts, and banners, and drums taken out of the funds is contrary to the Act, and, what's more," I says, "proceedings may be taken against you for paying away the funds for any such purpose, and I've a great mind to write to Mr Tidd Pratt about your doings at the Yorkshire Grey."

"Oh, bother Mr Tidd Pratt," he says, "I want to go to bed;" and with that he gets up and bolts out of the room, and up-stairs, and when I goes up, three minutes after, he is sprawling all over the bed, and snoring like a bull, and there was his clothes scattered over the room, and his money out of his waistcoat-pocket lying all about the floor. Now, I'm not one to search my husband's pockets, but when I find money lying about in that promiscuous manner, it's only natural that I should pick it up and count it. Well, there was three shillings in silver, half a screw of tobacco, and threepence-halfpenny in coppers, and, to my certain knowledge, when George went out to go to the Yorkshire Grey he had a bright half sovereign in his pocket; so that on that one lodge night he had spent six shillings and eightpence-halfpenny, which is very nigh five shillings over and above his subscription. So I don't wonder that he bolted away to bed, and wouldn't listen. That's where it is. They can't abear to be told the truth about their societies, for they know in their hearts that drink and drums is at the bottom of them.

It's my belief that if there were no public-houses there would be no Odd Fellows, and Foresters, and Ancient Druids, and other fools of the kind.

I've heard my brother John say, and now I believe it, that it's the badges, and the flags, and the bands of music that attracts members, just like recruiting for soldiers and slipping the shilling into poor young lads' hands, when they're dazzled with the ribbons and the fine uniform, and too much beer.

George was very fast in telling you all about his savings in the Post-office bank; but he didn't tell you that he once insured in the Bird-in-the-Hand Provident Association, and paid for two years, when the board was had up before the magistrate for swindling, and they broke into the office, and found it nothing but a back room at a corn-chandler's, with no furniture except three dirty tobacco-pipes and a beer can, which had been a missing from the public-house at the corner for months, and the chairman of the board, on being accused of it, took a bitter oath that he'd never seen the can, when he had been a using it all the time to boil his coffee.

The Bird-in-the-Hand gave out that it had five thousand pounds in the Bloomsbury Bank, but when they went and searched the books, they were told that it had only sixteen shillings there, and never had more than twenty pounds at any time. Whenever anybody died, the Bird-in-the-Hand disputed its liability, and the people were all too poor to make a stir about it, and have justice.

It's true George has got a bit of money laid by now, but what I'm afraid of is that he will be doing something foolish with it. I'm sure he's been bragging about his account out of doors, for there's scarce a day passes that he doesn't get letters wanting him to take shares in all kinds of companies and associations for the benefit of the working classes, and circulars besides from people that make regalia and badges, and banners, and satin aprons, and all such rubbish.

I read in my paper, which is the Penny Newsman, that Mr Gladstone is going to set up insurance offices for the working classes at the Post-office Savings-banks.* I hear that there's great opposition to it—by the publicans, I shouldn't wonder—but I'm sure if parliament was only composed of working men's wives the bill would be carried unanimously. It's just what the working man wants, for as things are now he doesn't know where to go for safety, and the way that lords and baronets and the aristocracy put their names to offices and societies, that never do anything but go into Chancery and wind up, is really shameful, and a snare to them as haven't got the education and knowledge to judge for themselves. I'm no politician myself, but, as a working man's wife

* This paper was written before the passing of the Government Annuities Act.

as knows how the money goes, I'm sure what Mr Gladstone proposes to do is good, and if he would only go a little further, and make the Post-offices sick funds as well, he will be the best friend the working classes ever had.

And bless him! I say, for the duty he has taken off the tea, and the bottle of brandy that you can now get at the grocer's, without sending the girl to the public-house, where the fellows get larking with her, leading to crinolines and red petticoats and ruin. Why, at Plumberry's, where I often buy my tea, we can now get brandy, gin, rum, and any kind of wine; and I'm sure, if George would only buy his bottle of rum there, and bring it home and have his glass by the fire-side with me (or a mate from the shop, too, if he likes), it would cost him less money; he would have no headache, and he'd be a deal more pleasant to all parties next morning.*

* This paragraph has been severely attacked by the teetotal organs, on the ground that it advocates drinking in grocers' shops. That is a misapprehension. If it advocates anything, it is the sale at grocers' shops of wholesome liquors, not to be drunk on the premises, but to be taken home and drunk there in moderation, away from the temptations of the public-house.

SHAKESPEARE NOT A MAN OF PARTS.

COMMEMORATE the birth of Shakespeare indeed! If you knew as much of Shakespeare as I do, or had suffered as much at his hands, you would curse the day that he ever was born. I tell you that Shakespeare has written more bad parts than any dramatic author living or dead. I ought to know, for I have been acting in his plays all my life, at least ever since I began to act, and that is when I was young and a fool, and didn't know better. I won't subscribe to his monument; there. Why should I? What has Shakespeare done for me? Done? Why, made my life a misery and a torment. Look at the parts he has written for me. There's Reynaldo, that's a pretty bit of character, isn't it?

"I will, my lord."
"My lord, I did intend it."
"Ay, very well, my lord."
"But, my lord."
"Ay, my good lord."
"Very well, my lord."

And you have to put on a velvet shirt and a pair of tights to say that. There's Rosencrantz and Guildenstern in the same play. A lively pair they are. I've played both—might have been put to double them, if that had been possible—and never got a hand for either. It's my belief that Shakespeare wrote the part of Rosencrantz to spite somebody. He's got nothing to do, and has some of the hardest sentences to speak in the whole play.

Try to get this into your head, and then when you have got it, try and speak it :

"The cease of majesty dies not alone; but, like a gulf, doth draw what's near it, with it: it is a massy wheel, fixed on the summit of the highest mount, to whose huge spokes ten thousand lesser things are mortised and adjoin'd; which, when it falls, each small annexment, petty consequence, attends the boisterous ruin."

That's Rosencrantz's best speech. Through one whole scene he has to stand with Guildenstern, like a knife and fork—that's what we call them in the country—and hasn't got a single word to say. In the scene following, his best point is,

"Ho, Guildenstern! bring in my lord."

And I should like to know if you think Osric worthy of an immortal bard!

"Your lordship is right welcome back to Denmark," he says.

"I thank your lordship, 'tis very hot."

"It is indifferent cold, my lord, indeed."

"I commend my duty to your lordship."

My opinion is that Osric is a muff. I'd rather play a policeman in a pantomime, and be bonneted. You say I am picking out one or two of the worst parts. Am I? What about Voltimand, Cornelius, Francisco, Fortinbras, Bernardo, Marcellus, the priest, and the captain? Why, there are eleven characters in this one play that are as bad as they can be. Not one of them ever gets a hand or a laugh. No dramatic author of the present day would dare to write such bad parts. Why, the very supers would strike at them, let alone general utility.

Take any play you like; one is as bad as another. The Merchant of Venice? What do you think are the feelings of an actor who has to buy a pair of new silk tights to play Salanio, or Salarino? They're both swells, and must wear silk tights; but they haven't a good line between them. A pretty thing, too, to have to dress yourself up for the Prince of Arragon, and find your own tights, hat, shoes, and jewelry. Once, when I was Prince of Morocco, I didn't have a dinner for a week, having been obliged to spend all my salary on the get up. Shakespeare, as an actor himself, ought to have known better than write such parts. Let me see what are the other characters in the play; Salerio, Leonardo, Balthazar, Stephano, and the Duke. I have played every one of them, and never could make anything of them—never knew any that could.

Macbeth better? Not a bit of it. Worse. What do you say to Lennox, Rosse, Menteth, Angus, Cathness, Fleance, Siward, old and young, the doctor, the bleeding officer, the porter, the old man? Why, it swarms with bad parts. Othello is not so bad; but yet you can't say there's much to be made out of the Duke of Venice and Ludovico.

There's only one merit in Shakespeare's dukes, and that is, that they generally sit at a table and don't show their legs. You may wear your street trowsers; only you must be careful to keep the tablecloth before you when you get up, so as not to show them. Take King John. I've played the King of France, but I must say a more ungrateful part I never dressed for; and a king too! Cardinal Pandulph is not worth a ——; well, if you object to the word, I'll say straw, which is weak, and doesn't half express my feelings.

I repeat, the Cardinal is not worth—allow me to say, a malediction, even when doubled with the Citizen of Angiers, who has to stand on a box with a tin pot on his head on the top of a pasteboard battlement, at the risk of his neck. I once went on for Cardinal Pandulph in a red frock and sugar-loaf hat, which is the correct thing, and somebody called out "Mother Shipton, by Jove!" and when I popped my head over the battlements afterwards as the Citizen, the boys in the gallery shallooed me. It is no joke, I can tell you, to be a cardinal one minute and a citizen on the top of a wall the next. And that is a pretty speech to put into a fellow's mouth, when he's balancing himself on an egg-box, with a weak board in the centre, and hanging on like grim death to a pasteboard wall, that wobbles about and threatens to come down with you every minute. It's a long speech, and it's a difficult speech, and very pleasant to deliver when King John is standing below swearing at you like a trooper because you don't give it right. Who could give it right? Just try this:

"If not complete, O, say he is not she; and she again wants nothing to name want, if want it be not, that she is not he; he is the half part of a blessed man, left to be finished by such a she, and she a fair divided excellence, whose fulness of perfection lies in him."

You don't recollect that passage? No, I should think not; who does? Nobody. If it wasn't Shakespeare you would say it was bosh.

And just imagine the citizen sliding down a ladder, to doff the tin pot and don the Mother Shipton hat to be ready for the next scene, where he walks in to "hail the anointed deputies of heaven," and demand why they spurn Mother Church and defy the Pope. It's not "once a priest, always a priest," when you play Pandulph, I can tell you. It's first one thing and then another, and when you are the Cardinal and when the citizen, you don't always know for certain.

As You Like it? No, I *don't* like it. Why, there are more bad parts in that play than I have fingers to count them on, including thumbs: Frederick, Amiens, Le Beau, Orlando, Dennis, Adam, Mar-text, Corin, Sylvius, Jaques. You call Jaques a good part, do you? Why he has only to come in at the end, and say,

"Let me have audience for a word or two; I am the second son of old Sir Rowland."

And then tell a long story about a boy and an old man, which nobody listens to. For my part, I always skip it, and when I have said that I am the second son of Sir Rowland, finish up at once with,

"This, to be true, I do engage my life."

You don't recollect that in Jaques's part? I do; and I don't remember much else. Do I mean the melancholy Jaques? I do mean the melancholy Jaques; he's melancholy enough, in all conscience.

"All the world's a stage, and all the men and women merely players"?

There's nothing of the kind in the part; I've played it often, and I ought to know. You mean that other Jaques. Oh, well; I have never played that, and if it ain't better than Jaques de Bois I don't want to. I tell you, you can't name a single one of Shakespeare's plays that ain't full of the very worst parts that ever were offered to an actor. And the worst of it is, that if you threaten to throw them up, you are told that you mustn't; for it's Shakespeare. And you are expected to take as much pains with them as if they were the finest things that ever were written.

It's pains thrown away; that's what I contend. Did you ever hear an audience applaud Cardinal Pandulph, or the First Citizen? Did you ever know a critic mention Ratcliffe or Catesby in his review? I have been acting Shakespearian parts now for thirty years, and I don't think I ever was mentioned but once, and that was when I made a mistake, and said,

"The early village cock hath thrice done solution to the morn."

And then the ill-natured critic congratulated

me upon the introduction of a new reading of the immortal bard.

He was not for an age, but for all time, you say. Worse luck. How his plays came down through three hundred years to this day, is a puzzle to me. And what's more puzzling, is all this fuss that you're making about their immortal author. You have been a long time making your minds up to give him a statue, and you set to work at last when his plays have gone out of fashion, and when people won't go to see them even with orders. Is it likely that anybody will go and see Balthazar, and Montano, and Rosencrantz, and Guildenstern? But you want to erect a statue to the author. Now, that's what I call inconsistent.

Will I go down to his birthplace? Certainly not. I know I should hate the very sight of it. What pleasure could it be to me to gaze upon the birthplace of a man who has left me nothing but an inheritance of bad parts? Why didn't he follow his father's trade, and be a woolstapler? If he had made stockings or blankets, and they'd been bad ones, they would only have troubled the people of his own time; they would have been worn out long before this. But his plays have lasted, confound them! Will I take a ticket for the actors' supper in his honour, price, to suit all classes of the profession, five shillings? No, I won't. Why should I? Shakespeare never gave me a five-shilling supper. Nothing like it. It's been mostly saveloys and a crust, with half a pint of porter. Rump-steak and onions at the best on ticket-nights. Go to the masked ball? I think I see myself; and have to buy, or hire, the rags to go in. No, I thank you; Shakespeare has cost me fancy dresses enough already. Would you have me get a new pair of silk tights, and go as Salanio; or hire a set of Bow-street jewels, and appear as the Prince of Morocco? Will I drink to the bard's memory on the day? No, I won't; but I'll tell you what I'll do; if *you* are inclined to be hospitable, I'll drink to *your* health now.

SHAKESPEARE-MAD.

I FEEL now, at this cool and collected moment, that for a whole week I have been going about with straws in my hair—a raving maniac. Here are the straws lying before me in a tangled wisp: a pewter medal, with an effigy in profile of the Immortal Bard on one side, and a front elevation view of his birthplace on the other; item, a triple badge in Coventry ribbon with the Bard's lineaments in floss silk, and woven representations of natal spot, and church containing dust; item, button with rosy-cheeked miniature of the Bard in enamel; item, blue scarf with full length Bard in an impossible but traditional attitude, pointedly calling attention to a scroll inscribed with a passage from his own works of which, I am led to infer, he was particularly proud.

Now, considering that for six days I have been rushing about in a frantic state of excitement with all these straws in my hair, I take it as highly generous on the part of my relatives that they have abstained from procuring the certificate of two qualified medical practitioners, and locking me up in Bedlam. When the mania seized upon me, I resolved to do two things which the Bard himself, in his profound philosophy, never could have dreamt of. I resolved to assist at the planting of a tree in London, and to be present at a display of fireworks in Stratford-upon-Avon, on one and the same day. I carried my resolve into execution. I was on Primrose-hill at three o'clock, and I was on the bridge at Stratford-upon-Avon at nine. But I had entered upon my mad career before this.

At the witching hour of the previous night, when the last stroke of twelve ushered in the natal day, I betook myself to a famous hostelrie to sup in the Bard's honour, in the exclusive company of the living illustrators of his works. I will not attempt to conceal that I was drawn thither, not altogether by reverence for the Bard, but, in some degree, by the expectation that certain of his illustrators would probably appear in the full evening costume of velvet tunics and russet boots with spurs. It was whispered that, on the transpontine shore, russet boots and spurs were considered the correct thing on such high festive occasions.

Let me silence whispering malice, and give the transpontine illustrators their due. If there were any there more spotless as to shirt fronts, more resplendent as to the polish of their patent leather boots, more completely *en règle* as to the dimensions of their white cravats, more fashionable as to the cut of their black dress-coats and pantaloons, more snowy as to the hue of their cambric handkerchiefs, than others, they were the illustrators from over the water. I will even go so far as to say that, as regards the oiliness of their hair, and the number of plaits on their shirt-fronts, they put the illustrators of the West End to shame and confusion.

When I found myself in their midst crushing up the broad stairs of the hostel, all classes and degrees mingling on equal terms of brotherhood in honour of the great High Priest of their art, it occurred to me that I was not doing such a very mad thing after all. Up they went, a strangely amalgamated crowd of leading tragedians and comedians, rubbing shoulders and exchanging friendly greetings with general utility, and supernumeraries, and pantomimists, and prompters, and call-boys, and even door-keepers. Ah, surely he was a Great Magician, whose name, after three centuries, could work such a charm. It was good for the heart to see such community of feeling, and curious to mark how unaccustomed they all were to the use of tickets of admission. None of them had their tickets ready, and when they were demanded by the man at the top of the stairs, the illustrators seemed to regard it as quite a joke that *they* should be asked for tickets, as if they were the public.

When they were all seated, the great hall was, as an illustrator in the eccentric line observed, "gorged with talent," which evoked from another the remark that it would be a fine thing for the country actors, longing for London, if the floor were to give way and entomb the lot. Happily, however, no such combination of good and bad luck occurred; though the enthusiasm at times was well calculated to inspire fears for the security of the roof. The unveiling of the statue of the Bard at the beginning of the feast, acted like a spark of fire upon a heap of gunpowder. The illustrators sprang to their feet and went off in one tremendous bang of applause. Yet there could scarcely have been twenty persons in that room who had much to be thankful to the Bard for. For four or five whom he had blessed with Macbeth, there were a hundred whom he had condemned to the carrying of banners. I had the pleasure of sitting beside a banner-bearer, one who had nailed his colours to the flagstaff in early life, and was resolved to stand by them to the last, and he was as enthusiastic as—nay, more enthusiastic than Macbeth, who, I am bound to say, devoted himself very closely to his supper, and took it coolly.

The name of Shakespeare, mention of the Player's Art, the Stage, were all so many sparks of fire falling upon gunpowder which never burned out, but always renewed itself from its own ashes and smoke to go off again and again with an explosion which shook the walls, and caused their Royal Highnesses the Dukes of Kent and Sussex to tremble in their gilt frames. So much enthusiasm and so much unity of feeling were probably never witnessed in any similar gathering.

Nothing but Shakespeare's wand could have ruled such an ocean, ordinarily agitated by so many diverse currents and disturbed by so many opposing winds. All jealousies and disappointments were laid aside for the time, and one feeling animated and controlled the vast assembly. Notwithstanding a little noisy disagreement—not about Shakespeare—which took place between two perfervid youths at the end of the room, this gathering of actors in honour of the great master of the dramatic art was, in its broad and general aspect, a most impressive spectacle. I, who had come with a strong predisposition to be amused, rather than impressed, was fain to confess this much. I could not think of any other class that would have been so unanimous and so hearty in an act of homage to a chief.

And so, when they had lingered to the last, loth to tear themselves away from a scene of such rare enjoyment, in the bright sunshine on the morning of Shakespeare's three hundredth birthday, the players streamed out into the street, while citizens, awakened possibly from dreams of last night's play, peered at them from the corners of blinds, and utterly failed to recognize Falstaff in the respectable cleanly gentleman gaily jumping into a Hansom cab; or Bardolph in the smart young man with the embroidered shirt-front; or King Henry IV. in the tall gentleman in the black surtout, borrowing a light for his cigar from Francis, the drawer, in all the magnificence of a white hat resplendent in the morning sun.

Surely I am mad now, for I go away in a four-wheeled cab in company with Hamlet, Prince of Denmark, and Horatio his friend, and the First Gravedigger, who has only one waistcoat on, and that bound with gold braid, and the Ghost of Hamlet's father outside on the box, scenting the morning air with a briar-root pipe, away to the north-western regions, where early shop-keeping birds are taking down their shutters, and preparing to catch the first human worms that appear above-ground—away in the fresh morning air, until we begin to persuade ourselves that we are not tired, and that there is no necessity to go to bed.

We do not go to bed, but joyfully accept an invitation to breakfast with First Gravedigger, whose pressing hospitality at that awkward hour in the morning is an astonishment to us all, until he informs us that the partner of his bosom is out of town; which fully accounted, I will not say for the milk in the cocoa-nut, but for the coffee with boiling milk, accompanied by hot rolls and a cold capon—I will not say fowl in this connection—with which we were presently refreshed. Passed several hours in a ridiculous attempt to be lively and wide awake, and just giving it up and sinking into the arms of Morpheus and an easy-chair, when the Ghost of Hamlet's Father, who is used to late hours, cries out, "More Shakespeare!" and we all start to our feet, and find, on consulting the dials in our pokes, that it is time to hie us to the Oak.

So away we go through the gate, and past a cluster of genteel villas, to the base of the mountain, whereon a number of flying merchants and perambulating speculators have seized the occasion to revive the glories of Chalk Farm fair. Oi Polloi in great force, vox populi very loud, harshly and hoarsely inviting us to eat oranges—though that was not particularly enjoined if we only bought them—to drink sherbet, to have a shie at a cocoa-nut three sticks a penny, to treat ourselves to an electric shock, to try our weight, to buy gingerbread-nuts. Some confusion of ideas apparent with respect to the occasion. Shakespeare a good deal mixed up with Garibauldy. Boys, evidently unable to grapple with the subject in hand, give vent to their general feelings in the exclamation, "Whoop, Shakepeare!" which may, or may not, have been intended to be complimentary. I perceive that the tree has been already planted, but there is no great sensation in its immediate neighbourhood.

The flying merchants and the perambulating speculators cannot complain that the Bard is exercising any superior attraction. He isn't. Populace cannot be induced to pay a shilling for admission to the enclosure round the tree. If there is anything that is considered not for an age, but for all time, it is the game of three sticks a penny. Some slight sensation, but not much, when Mr Phelps is brought along, a man on each side of him, holding him fast by the arms. It occurs to me that Mr Phelps is in custody, and that the two men are policemen in plain clothes—very plain clothes, I may remark—taking him off to the station. I follow, intending to offer myself as bail, and try to catch the tragedian's mournful eye, but he is evidently ashamed of himself, and does not wish to be recognized; so I spare his feelings, and remain to review the procession, which consists of six men and a boy, the last carrying a brown paper parcel, which a youth of an inquiring mind, who turns himself upside down to read the inscription on the cover, informs me contains the "hode."

I followed Mr Phelps with my eyes until I saw him dragged into the station-house and confronted with the inspector, who immediately took down the charge, the two officers in plain clothes evidently asseverating that the tragedian had assaulted them in the execution of their duty, and had been very obstropolous and voilent. What they did with him after that, I cannot say, and few apparently cared to know; for, after the procession passed, the populace resumed the shieing of three sticks, and cracked nuts, and weighed itself, and took electric shocks, and generally dispersed itself over the hill, out of sight of the Oak, and out of hearing of the Ode.

In the comfortable belief that I had seen all and done my duty, I now turned my steps homewards, but had not proceeded far when I heard the strains of martial music, and presently came upon a small army of Foresters marching on to the field, like the Prussians at Waterloo, a little late in the day. I understand that at this moment Mr Phelps was standing with his watch in his hand, wishing that either Chaos or the Foresters were come. That the Foresters were late seemed to be entirely owing to their zeal and love of glory, for they insisted upon bringing the banner of the Bard of Avon lodge with them, and the banner being large, requiring two poles, and the wind contrary, the army, which, in respect of its mainsail, seemed to be one of foot-marines, made rather a slow march, or rather voyage, of it.

That its progress had been an arduous and disastrous one, became painfully evident to me as I proceeded onward. All along the road I encountered stray Foresters, who had fallen out of the ranks, overcome by fatigue and—as they were generally showing their exhaustion in close proximity to a public-house — possibly beer. One gentleman in a full suit of Lincoln green, and a hat with three exhausted feathers, was being danced round by a little circle of boys and girls, who seemed to have some vague notions that he might be Shakespeare, or at any rate some celebrity deserving of honour. This is the last glimpse I have of the celebration in London.

In little more than three hours after I am at the little station at Stratford-upon-Avon, in company with about a dozen others, who are all the pilgrims who have come by the G. W. R. that evening to worship at the shrine. As I had never visited Stratford before, I declined a conveyance, and walked into the town, prepared to feel that I was treading sacred ground, and to be much moved by all I saw. I expected to come upon "the House" suddenly, and I felt sure I should know it from its portraits. Every now and then I thought I saw it looming in the distance, and began to feel a thrill, but I was mistaken again and again, and the thrill subsided—subsided past recall, when I suddenly found myself in front of a yellow caravan, where they were exhibiting waxwork and a Scotch giant. This diverted my thoughts. I began to think of the pushing character of the people north of the Tweed, who had sent this Scotch giant to compete with the great English giant on his own ground and on his own natal day. Certainly the Scotch giant had the best of it in one respect. He was alive, O! alive!

Not coming upon the house fortuitously, as I expected, I thought it prudent—particularly as I had heard alarming accounts of the great influx of pilgrims, and the scarcity of accommodation—to look out for an hotel. Found one in the principal street, and was asked a guinea a night for a bed. Explained that I was not Baron Rothschild, and was informed that I might have one higher up for half a guinea; consented to this, and had a momentary impression that I must be very rich; and that hitherto I had been regulating my expenditure on a scale altogether unbefitting my means. Could not rest for refreshment or anything, until I had seen the House; so immediately sallied out in search of it, trying to forget the yellow caravan and the Scotch giant. Did not like to inquire my way to the House; felt that I ought to be drawn to it by an influence; and that it would show a want of delicacy and veneration to ask any one to show it me, as if it were a bank or a post-office, or something of that sort.

Stratford was not so large a town but that I might easily find the shrine which was its pride and glory, its sacred place. The paths worn with pilgrims' feet should direct me to it. I assure you I had got over the Scotch giant, and was fully primed with the right feeling. I have the bump of veneration strongly developed. Vestiges of antiquity, relics of great men, places with classic associations, interest and move me deeply. I never pass through Temple Bar and take a walk down Fleet-street without thinking of Johnson and Goldsmith, and picturing them in my mind's eye. I had long looked forward to this day; long promised myself a visit to Stratford; many a time and oft had visited it in imagination, and realized all the sensations which its associations are calculated to inspire. And I was prepared to realize all these feelings now with tenfold intensity. But I could not find the House, and was obliged to ask my way to it after all. It is a fact, that the person to whom I applied for guidance looked puzzled, and turned first this way and then that, and at last confessed that he "really didn't know where the House was situated." He was apparently an intelligent man, in the cattle-dealing line, I fancy; but he had an excuse for his ignorance in so insignificant a matter—he had been only a fortnight in Stratford!

"Down there, sir, on the right-hand side of the way," said a native.

I was thankful for the first part of the direction, but I did not want him to tell me on which side of the way; I wanted to find that out for myself, and I escaped hastily, lest the native should spoil my pleasure by pointing at the house with a showman's finger, and saying, "That's it!" I knew now that I was coming to it, and that a few more paces would bring me to it. I was approaching it with all reverence, and with a feeling that the thrill was about to rise, when the sky was suddenly illuminated by a flash of bright light, accompanied by a peculiar rushing noise in the air. I was not left for a single moment in doubt as to the cause. I looked up, and saw that it was a rocket. They were letting off fireworks in the neighbouring meadow! A few more steps and I was in front of the House, and *I saw it for the first time by the light of fireworks!* The thrill did not rise. By the garish light of red and blue and green fires I saw a house which had been restored out of all its antiquity, which was trim and neat, and angular, and varnished, and which, when the rockets exploded and rained down their spray of coloured fires, and the people shouted in the meadow, recalled a vision of Vauxhall. The general tea-garden aspect of the house was disappointing enough, but with the accompaniment of fireworks the effect was shockingly depressing. There was so much of the tea-garden about the place, that I should not have been at all surprised if some one had appeared at the window, sung a comic song, and asked conundrums. Indeed, on returning presently through the deserted street—there was not a soul in it beside myself on this evening of the Tercentenary—I heard the sound of minstrelsy proceeding from a public-house, and, looking through the window, I beheld a busker in the costume of the music-hall Irishman, dancing a jig and singing Limerick Races, while the townsmen of Shakespeare sat around and drank beer, and smoked pipes, and did homage to the Bard!

I knew that I should never feel the thrill after this. The restorer and the fireworks had done for me. So I went in for the display of fireworks pure and simple, and thought it, per se, not so very bad.

A few flags fluttering about the pretty little town, but no commotion until after the fireworks, when a dense crowd of yokels breaks into the streets, like an inundation of muddy water. Heedless, blundering yokels, with tremendous feet, who run against you, and stamp upon you, and scent the air with fustian and corduroy. Away they go, following the band, and when the band has blown itself out they disperse themselves among the little taverns, which seem to be in the proportion of one to three of the houses, and the streets are quiet and deserted again.

Revisited the House on Sunday morning, hoping to see it under more favourable circumstances. Well, there were no fireworks, and the new beams and laths let into the house did not look so varnished and glittering by daylight. Peeped in at one of the windows, never imagining that I would be admitted on that day, when a person immediately ran out and pounced upon me. Would I walk up? but first my sixpence.

I paid my sixpence, and walked up; but here again my pleasure was marred. The work of renovation had not been extended to the natal chamber, and I could well believe that no alteration had been made in it since Shakespeare's time; but it was occupied by two huge Warwickshire policemen in full uniform, whose presence was suggestive of a murder, or a robbery, or something of a similar nature requiring the superintendence of the authorities.

I could have been much impressed by those old worm-eaten boards, which Shakespeare's feet had trod, but who could adore a sacred spot with two policemen standing at his elbow, irreverently lounging against the walls, and blowing their noses like thunder in great sheets of red calico? Could not remain and muse in such company; so looked hurriedly round at the countless names scribbled all over the walls and ceiling, noticing "Walter Scott" awkwardly scratched on one of the diamond panes of the window, and rendered almost illegible by the names of Brown and Jones and Robinson that had been scrawled through it, over it, under it, and all about it; saw also the name of Thackeray neatly written in pencil on the ceiling, the place nearest his hand; and observed generally that the names that were written in the largest characters and in the most conspicuous places, were those of ladies and gentlemen from the United States of America.

Paid another sixpence to the Museum, where I saw many interesting things, including Shakespeare's ring, which he must have worn on his thumb; the desk at which he sat at school, and on which he had only partly accomplished the carving of his initials, having been unable, apparently, to turn the tail of the S, leaving it in the condition of a C; many documents of the period, one relating to house property, with John Shakespeare, his mark (a very unsteady cross), at the foot of it; a letter to the poet from a friend in London, asking him for the loan of thirty pounds —the only epistle extant addressed to the poet; a large folio manuscript book, recently discovered in the Lord Chamberlain's office, in which Shakespeare is mentioned at the head of a list of other players, as having received "iiij yardes of skarlet red cloth," to enable him to appear in a procession on the occasion of the entry of King James into London; a flat candlestick found at the bottom of the well in New Place, the site of the Bard's grand house, a candlestick with which he may often have gone up to bed, and which, having been found at the bottom of a well, I am inclined to regard as a true relic; much mulberry and many clay pipes of modern aspect, which I reject altogether.

From the house to the church, where I deem myself fortunate in finding a seat in the chancel exactly opposite the Bard's monument. I am afraid I paid more attention to the bust than to the service. The effigy struck me very much, and gave me quite a new idea of the Bard's features and expression. Give me this bust, and I resign to you all the portraits. I have here the counterfeit presentment of a face suggestive above all things of strong vitality, freshness of spirit, and liveliness of disposition. I can imagine this to be the face of a man who was full of natural genius and did not know it; whose animal and mental spirits never flagged; who never toiled at anything; whose head never ached.

I cannot discuss the question of the plaster cast of the face, said to have been taken after death, and used as a model by the artist who executed this effigy. I can only say that the effigy satisfies me, and that I can believe Shakespeare to have been exactly such a man as it represents. I am in a very favourable position in the chancel for making these observations and revolving these thoughts, but not for hearing the Archbishop of Dublin's sermon, which is preached far away up in the body of the church from a pulpit which I cannot see. Every now and then, however, I hear the word "Shakespeare," and catch portions of familiar quotations from his works, and, straining my ear, I hear the archbishop say by way of peroration, that Shakespeare was a gift from Heaven, for which we ought to give thanks. And after a three hours' sederunt, we stream out of the beautiful church, and march home to our dinners (getting cold) to the martial strains of the town band; and as I keep step to "See the conquering hero," I wonder if Exeter Hall is present, and what he is thinking of all this.

I walk across the fields in the evening to Ann Hathaway's cottage, and am charmed with the quiet rural beauty of the scene. The fields are sparkling with daisies and wild flowers, like stars in a firmament of green; the rooks are cawing high up on the trees; the groves are ringing with the songs of birds; the air is laden with the perfume of new leaves. That long-expected thrill comes unbidden now. Truly a place to nurse a poet. I sit lingering upon every stile, drawing in great draughts of the fresh exhilarating air, as if I could take in a stock of it to last me when I have returned to the murky city. And by-and-by little maidens come round me with offerings of bunches of daisies and cowslips, with a view to halfpence—and when I inquire the whereabouts of the cottage, they all volunteer to be my guides; and remonstrance and halfpence being equally in vain, I proceed onwards escorted by a whole troop of maidens, who seem to conduct me in triumph.

I find the cottage more real than the house; no paint and varnish here; but all the old beams, many of the old stones, and a thatched roof that might be an age. A female descendant of the Hathaways receives me at the door joyfully, and conducts me through the apartments—the sitting-room and kitchen combined, where I imagined William and Ann sitting courting on the stone ledge under the great chimney—if, indeed, Ann's father ever allowed the lad to come beyond the garden-gate—up-stairs to the bedroom, where Ann probably arrayed herself in bridal attire previous to proceeding on William's arm to Luddington church.

And here there is a wonderful old bedstead of black oak, which I imagined might be that "second-best" which the Bard bequeathed to his widow. The female descendant of the Hathaways could not say: perhaps it might be. Express myself very much pleased with the cottage, and descendant of the Hathaways hopes I will tell my friends that the show is worth seeing. On looking at the visitors' book I can understand her anxiety in this respect. Very few pilgrims have as yet walked across the fields to view Ann Hathaway's cottage. I return by the way I came, and find a missionary preaching under a hedge to a select congregation of rustics, denouncing the established clergy, especially in the form of archbishops, calling down vengeance upon the Pavilion, and describing Shakespeare as a worm.

The expected influx of visitors from all corners of the earth did not take place at the beginning of the week, as the natives fondly hoped; and sleeping became a less expensive luxury. Beds declined in the market, and sofas that had been looking up on Saturday, were entirely at a discount. Omnibuses came rattling up from the station with only three or four persons in them. Wombwell's menagerie came in with a little village of yellow vans and many men and horses, looked about and thought it would go away again. Eventually, however, drew up beside the Scotch giant, and blew brass horns until it was black in the face; but to no purpose. Performing elephants were reported to be engaged in an entirely new and astonishing feat—that of eating their heads off. I call at the office of the committee, and find that a poet has sent in an invocation beginning:

Come let us Tereentenerate—

Wander forth again and invoke the town in the poet's words: Come let us tercentenerate, by all means. But at present all the tercentenerating is done by the town band, which for wind is a paragon. The performance of the Messiah at the Pavilion in the afternoon is, as respects the attendance, a failure. The audience consisted chiefly of the gentry of the neighbourhood, who came in their carriages and went away again immediately the performance was over.

It was a bitter sight for the natives to see the horses eating out of their own nose-bags, and the owners of the horses sitting in the carriages eating out of *their* own nose-bags—not patronizing the town to the extent of a feed of corn, nor a biscuit and a glass of sherry. Prospect brightens, however, on Tuesday, when the players come. Tickets for Twelfth Night going off rapidly, and the indefatigable mayor, who is ubiquitous, begins to look more cheerful. The vicar, beloved of all the natives high and low, is seen driving through the town a phaeton, in which are seated side by side the Bishop of St Andrews and Sir Andrew Aguecheek, the bishop craving for something more solid than Twelfth Night, and asking Sir Andrew why he doesn't play Macbeth.

I go to the Pavilion for the first time to see the comedy, and am delighted with the splendid proportions of the building; consider it a model of what a theatre ought to be, and can only account for its perfection by the supposition that the architect set to work to construct a wooden tent and by accident hit upon a perfect theatre. The Pavilion is larger in area than any theatre in London, and yet the spectator can see and hear in every part of it, and this seems to be owing to the low roof and the absence of piled-up tiers of boxes. Will some one confer a great obligation on the London play-going public by bringing the Pavilion up to London, and planting it, say, in Leicester-Square?

Sitting in a wide open balcony, with plenty of room to move about, and neither oppressed with heat nor chilled with draughts of cold air, I thought Twelfth Night a more enjoyable comedy than I had ever thought it before, and considered that I had never seen it so well played even by the Haymarket company: which impressions, I have no doubt, were induced by the beauty and the comfort of the theatre. I had seen all the plays and all the actors, but I went night after night simply to enjoy the rare English luxury of being comfortable in a theatre.

Now that the players were coming down every day, there was an agreeable combination of the rus in urbe, of London and Stratford, about the place. When I had heard the band blow from all quarters of the town, and marched hither and thither, always turning into Henley-street to see the House, and never finding anybody near it, except on one occasion, when Punch was giving his performance exactly opposite; when I had mused myself nearly asleep in the old churchyard, or by the banks of the placid Avon; when I had inspected the portraits of the Bard in the Town-hall, and the plaster cast with some hairs adhering to the moustache, concerning which I had grave doubts, and the walking-stick and drinking-cup under the glass case, and more pipes from New Place: and gazed in through a window at an old rusty piece of iron, said to be the original key of the church where Shakespeare was married; and dropped in for a glass of ale at the Falcon, whose parlour is lined with the oak panelling from the Bard's grand house, and where the Bard himself is said to have sat of an evening and smoked a pipe, to the wonder and amazement of the village gossips—when I had done all these things, and tercentenerated (poet, I thank thee for that word!) to my heart's content, it was very pleasant to betake me to a certain snug room in the Red Horse, there to foregather with Sir Andrew Aguecheek and Sir Toby Belch, and Malvolio, and the two Dromios, and Touchstone, and many more, who were well bestowed at that hostel, when they were not being entertained by the most hospitable Mayor and the no less hospitable Vicar. And here, whenever a new comer arrived, Washington Irving's poker was brought in, tenderly encased in a blue baize sheath, and handed round to be admired. Washington Irving had stirred the fire with that very poker, in that very room, and so it has been a holy poker ever since. And here the Irish "busker" stole in one evening and gave us a recitation with remarkable emphasis and propriety, showing that, when occasion required, he had a soul above Limerick Races and Irish jigs.

Away on the top of an omnibus to Charlcote Park, the scene of the Bard's poaching exploit. An unbelieving phantom who has haunted me for days, and denied the birthplace, and the tomb, and everything else, now denies the poaching. I shut him up finally, by myself denying Shakespeare altogether. After a three miles' ride, we come upon the park, which is swarming with tame deer, and I picture young Will sneaking under the shadow of the wall to knock one of them on the head. Seeing that the deer are all as tame as hens or ducks, it came into my head that it was not poaching, but something else, which I will not mention. Drive up to the new gate, beside which is preserved an old post, which we are left to imagine is the very post on which the youthful poet fixed his lampoon upon Sir Thomas. And now a strange thought. The house and park of the Lucys are thrown open to visitors to-day in the name of one who once did the family the honour to steal a deer from its park.

If the story be not true, it is still more remarkable that a slander in connection with the Bard's name should have been enough to immortalize a house, and render a family famous. The house and grounds very beautiful—the gardens laid out to realize a picture by Watteau: the house reminding one of the magnificence of Versailles—oak floors, emblazoned ceilings, and the walls hung with rare pictures by old masters. The portrait of Sir Thomas Lucy over the mantelpiece, and the marble monument in the church, forbid the idea of Justice Shallow. They are emphatically the portraits of a gentleman—a chivalrous-looking gentleman, with a fine head and a noble countenance.

Returning over the old bridge to Stratford, I am horrified to see the calm bosom of the Avon being ruffled by the paddle-wheels of a dirty steamboat from the Birmingham Soho. Man on the bank touting for passengers to go up the river to Luddington, where the Bard was married. I have seen his birthplace, and I have seen his tomb, and I should like to view the scene of the middle event of his life; but I decline to navigate the Avon in a steamboat, so forego Luddington, and content myself with another sight of the old key in the shop window in High-street.

Now, if you ask me if I passed a pleasant time and enjoyed myself, I answer that I passed a very pleasant time, and never enjoyed myself more in my life. Nature has made the neighbouring country a paradise of quiet beauty, and the mayor and the committee, as the representatives of Art, certainly did everything in their power to add to the delights of the town. The erection of that handsome Pavilion I regard as a great achievement, and too much praise cannot be awarded to the committee for its spirit and enterprise in providing entertainments utterly regardless of expense.

As an example, the whole of the scenery and properties that were used in Romeo and Juliet at the Princess's Theatre, on Tuesday night, in London, were used in Stratford on Wednesday, and were seen again in London on the evening of Thursday. I think, as a whole, the celebration was as successful as could have been reasonably expected. The Pavilion was never filled, but it would have been difficult to fill so large a building even in London. If the visitors from the neighbourhood came and went away again the same day without spending money in the town, the natives had only themselves to blame. Thousands were scared away by the false reports of overcrowded hotels and high charges. But that honour to the Bard had much to do with the celebration, I will not pretend to declare, in the face of the fact, that the most successful entertainment in the Pavilion, specially erected for the purpose of performing his works, was a masked ball.

DOCTOR GOLIATH.

How the Doctor found his way into our society, none of us can tell. It did not occur to us to inquire into the matter at the time, and now the point is lost in the dim obscurity of the past. We only know that he appeared suddenly and mysteriously. It was shortly after we had formed our Mutual Admiration Society, in this very room in Mrs. Lirriper's Lodgings. We were discussing things in general in our usual amiable way, admiring poets, worshipping heroes, and taking all men and all things for what they seemed. We were young and ingenuous, pleased with our own ideas, and with each other's; full of belief and trust in all things good and noble, and with no hatred, save for what was false, and base, and mean. In this spirit we were commenting with indignation upon a new heresy with regard to the age of the world, when a strange voice broke in upon our conversation.

"I beg your pardon; you are wrong. The age of the world is exactly three millions, eight hundred and ninety-seven thousand, four hundred and twenty-five years, eight months, fourteen days, nine hours, thirty-five minutes, and seventeen seconds."

At the first sound of this mysterious voice we all looked up, and perceived standing on the hearth-rug before the fire by which you sit, Major, a little closely-knit, middle-aged man, dressed in black. He had a hooked nose, piercing black eyes, and a grizzled beard, and his head was covered with a shock of crisp dark hair. Our first impulse was to resent the stranger's interference as an impertinence, and to demand what business he had in that room in Mrs Lirriper's house, sacred to the social meetings of the Mutual Admiration Society? But we no sooner set eyes upon him than the impulse was checked, and we remained for a minute or so gazing upon the stranger in silence.

We saw at a glance that he was no mere meddling fool. He was considerably older than any of us there present, his face beamed with intelligence, his eyes sparkled with humour, and his whole expression was that of a man confident of mental strength and superiority. The look on his face seemed to imply that he had reckoned us all up in an instant. So much were we impressed by the stranger's appearance, that we quite forgot the queries which had naturally occurred to us when he interrupted our conversation: Who are you? Where do you belong to? How did you come here? It was allowable for a member of the society to introduce a friend; but none of us had introduced him, and we were the only members in the room. None of us had seen him enter, nor had we been conscious of his presence until we heard his voice.

On comparing notes afterwards, it was found that the same thought had flitted across all our minds. Had he come down the chimney? Or up through the floor? But at the time, as we saw no smoke and smelt no brimstone, we dismissed the suspicion for the more natural explanation that some member had introduced him, and had gone away, leaving him there. I was mentally framing a civil question with the view of elucidating this point, when the stranger, who spoke with a foreign accent, again addressed us.

"I trust," he said, "I am not intruding upon your society; but the subject of your discussion is one that I have studied deeply, and I was betrayed into a remark by—by my enthusiasm: I beg you will pardon me."

He said this so affably, and with so much dignified politeness of an elderly kind, that we were all disarmed, and protested, in a body, that there was no occasion for any apology. And it followed upon this, in some sort of insensible way, that the stranger came and took a seat among us, and spent the evening with us, proving a match for us in the airy gaiety of our discussions, and more than a match for us in all kinds of knowledge. We were all charmed with the stranger, and he appeared to be highly pleased with us. When he went away he shook hands with us with marked cordiality and warmth, and left us his card. It bore this inscription:

DOCTOR GOLIATH, PH.D.

After this the doctor regularly frequented our society, and we took his coming as a matter of course; being quite content to accept his great learning and numerous accomplishments as a certificate of his eligibility for membership in our fraternity. It was no wonder that we came to look upon the doctor as a great personage. His fund of knowledge was inexhaustible. He seemed to know everything—not generally and in a superficial manner—but particularly and minutely.

It was not, however, by making a parade of his knowledge that he gave us this impression. He let it out incidentally, as occasion required. If language were the topic, the doctor, by a few off-hand remarks, made it plain to us that he was acquainted with almost every language under the sun. He spoke English with an accent which partook of the character of almost every modern tongue. If law came up, he could discourse of codes and judgments with the utmost familiarity, citing act, chapter, and section, as if the whole study of his life had been law. So with politics, history, geology, chemistry, mechanics, and even medicine. Nothing came amiss to Doctor Goliath. He was an animated Cyclopædia of universal knowledge.

But there was nothing of the pedant about him. He treated his learning as bagatelle; he threw off his knowledge as other people throw off jokes; he was only serious when he mixed a salad, brewed a bowl of punch, or played a game of piquet. He was not at all proud of being able to translate the Ratcatcher's Daughter into six languages, including Greek and Arabic; but he believed he was the only man on the face of the earth who knew the exact proportions of oil and vinegar requisite for the proper mixture of a potato-salad. It was impossible to resist the spell of Doctor Goliath's wonderful character. He was learned in the highest degree; yet he had all the reckless jollity of a schoolboy, and could talk nonsense and make sport of wisdom and philosophy better than any of us. He took our society by storm; he became an oracle; we quoted him as an authority, and spoke of him as *the* doctor, as if there were no other doctor on the face of the earth.

Shortly before the doctor's appearance among us, we, the members of the Mutual Admiration Society, had sworn eternal friendship. We had vowed ever to love each other, ever to believe in each other, ever to be true and just and kindly towards each other, and never to be estranged one from another either by prosperity or adversity. As a sign and symbol of our brotherhood, we have agreed to call each other by familiar and affectionate abbreviations of our Christian names; and in pursuance of this amiable scheme, we had arranged to present each other with loving cups. As we were a society of little wealth, except in the matter of loving kindness and mutual admiration, it was resolved that the cups should be fashioned of pewter, of the measure of one quart, and each with two handles. The order was given, the loving-cups were made, and each bore an inscription in this wise: "To Tom from Sam, Jack, Will, Ned, Charley, and Harry, a token of Friendship;" this inscription being only varied as regarded the relative positions of donors and recipient. The cups were all ready, and nothing remained to be done but to pay the money and bring them away from the shop of our Benvenuto

Cellini, which was situated in the parish of St Martin's-in-the-Fields. A delay, however, occurred, owing to circumstances which I need not particularize further than to say, that they were circumstances over which we had no control.

This delay, owing to the obduracy of these uncontrollable circumstances, continued for some weeks, when, one evening, Tom came in with a large brown paper parcel under his arm. It was a parcel of strange and unwonted aspect.

"Ha! ha!" cried the doctor, "what have we here? Say, my Tom, is it something to eat, something to drink, something perchance to smoke? For in such things only doth my soul delight."

"I don't believe you when you say that, doctor," said Tom, quite seriously; for Tom had fallen more prostrate than any of us before the doctor's great character.

"Not believe me?" cried the doctor. "I mean it. Man, sir, is an animal whose only misfortune is, that he is endowed with the accursed power of thinking. If I were not possessed by this evil spirit of Thought, do you know what I would do?"

Tom could form no idea what he would do.

"Well, then," said the doctor, "I would lie

all day in the sun, and eat potato-salad out of a trough!"

"What! like a pig?" Tom exclaimed.

"Yes, like a pig," said the doctor. "I never see a pig lying on clean straw, with his snout poked into a delightful mess of barley-meal and cabbage leaves, but I become frightfully envious!"

"Oh, doctor," we all exclaimed in chorus.

"Fact. I say to myself, how much better off, how much happier, is this pig than I! To obtain my potato-salad, without which life would be a blank, I have to do a deed my soul abhors. I have to work. The pig has no work to do for that troughful of barley-meal and cabbage-leaves. Because I am an animal endowed with the power of thought and reason, I was sent to school and taught to read. See what misfortune, what misery, that has brought upon me! You laugh, but am I not driven to read books, and parliamentary debates, and leading articles? I was induced the other day to attend a social congress. If I had been a pig, I should not have had to endure that."

"Ah, but, doctor," said Tom, "the pig has no better part."

The doctor burst into a yell of exultation.

"What! The pig no better part? Ha! ha!

Sir, the better part of pig is pork. The butcher comes to me and to the pig alike; but what remains of me when he has done his fell work? You put me in a box and screw me down, and stow me away out of sight; and you pretend to grieve for me. But the pig—you eat him, and rejoice in earnest! And that reminds me that I shall have a pork-chop for supper. By the way, is it a lettuce you have in that paper parcel, Tom?"

"It is not a lettuce, doctor."

"Not a lettuce! Ha! I see something glitter—precious metal—gold? no, silver! to obtain which, in a commensurate quantity, I would commit crimes—murder!"

"Oh, doctor," said Tom, "you are giving yourself a character which you don't deserve."

"Am I?" said the doctor. "You don't know me. And after all, what is murder? Nothing. You kill two or three of your fellow-creatures—a dozen for that matter; what then? There are plenty more. Do you know what is the population of the earth? I will tell you. Exactly one thousand three hundred millions, eight hundred and ninety-nine thousand, six hundred and twenty souls. How many murders are committed in the course of a year, do you imagine? You think only those you read of in the newspapers. Bah! An intimate knowledge of the subject enables me to inform you that the number of murders committed in Great Britain and Ireland, and the Channel Islands, annually, amounts to fifteen thousand, seven hundred and forty-five. It is one of the laws of nature for keeping down the population. Every man who commits a murder obeys this law."

Tom's hair was beginning to stand on end, for the doctor said all this with a terrible fierceness of manner. His strange philosophy was not without its effect upon the rest of us. We had been accustomed to a good deal of freedom in our discussions, but we had never ventured upon anything so audacious as this.

"Come, Tom," said the doctor, "unveil your treasure, and let me see if it be worth my while lying in wait for you in the dark lanes as you go home to-night."

"Well, no, it isn't, doctor," said Tom, "for the article is only of pewter." And Tom uncovered his loving-cup. Circumstances had relented in Tom's case, and he had gone and paid for his own loving-cup.

"Pewter," said the doctor. "Bah! it is not worth my while; but if it had been silver, now, why then I might——" And the doctor put on a diabolical expression, that seemed to signify highway robbery accompanied with violence, and murder followed by immediate dissection. Presently the doctor noticed the inscription.

"Ha! ha!" he said, "what is this? An inscription! 'To Tom, from Sam, Jack, Will, Ned, Charley, and Harry — a token of Friendship.' Friendship? Ha! ha! 'tis but a name, an empty name, a mockery, a delusion, and a snare. I tell you there is no such thing in the world."

"Oh, don't say that, doctor!" cried Tom, looking quite hurt.

"Ah," returned the doctor, "you will find it out. I have always found it out; and since I formed my first friendship and was deceived—it is now—let me see how many years?—one thousand eight hundred and—but no matter."

The doctor paused, as if oppressed with painful recollections.

"Ned," said Sam, leaning across to me, "do you know what I think the doctor is?"

"No," I said.

"Well," he said, "hang'd if I don't think he is the Wandering Jew. Look at his boots!"

I looked at his boots. They were not neat boots: that was all I perceived about them.

"Don't you observe," said Sam, "how flat and trodden down they are? The doctor has done a deal of walking in those boots. Mark their strange and ancient shape! Look at the dust upon them—it is the dust of centuries!"

The doctor was roaring with laughter at the idea of our mutual presentation scheme, and was calling us "innocents," and Tom's loving-cup a "mug."

Tom was getting red in the face, and looking ashamed. In fact, we were all looking rather sheepish; for it had never struck us until now, how silly and sentimental we all were. We said nothing to the doctor about the six other loving-cups that were waiting to be paid for and claimed; and when Tom, with a face as red as a coal, covered up his "mug," as the doctor called it, and put it away, we were glad to change the subject, to escape from our embarrassment. We were so thoroughly ashamed of ourselves, that we endeavoured to redeem our characters in the eyes of the doctor, by plunging recklessly into any depth of cynical opinion that he chose to sound. And the doctor, in the course of time, led us to the very bottom of the pit of cynicism.

As we listened to him, and held converse with him day after day, we began to see how very green and unsophisticated we had all been. We came to know that the poets and heroes whom we had worshipped were nothing but humbugs and pretenders; that the great statesmen whom we had believed in and admired, were blunderers or traitors; that the mighty potentates whose power and sagacity we had extolled, were tyrannical miscreants, or puppets in the hands of others; that the philanthropists whom all men praised, were conceited self-seeking hypocrites; that the patriots whose names we had reverenced in common with all the world, were scoundrels of the deepest dye. The doctor's influence led us on insensibly, step by step. How could we resist it? It was a fascination. He knew everything, could prove everything, and had such a store of facts that we had never heard of in support of his conclusions, that it was impossible, with our limited knowledge, to withstand him. We were shocked at first; but, as the revolution proceeded, we got used to the sight of blood, and saw the heads of our heroes fall, with the utmost indifference. At length we came to revel in it, and sought for new victims, that we might demolish them and do our despite upon them. The doctor led the way more boldly as we advanced. He hinted darkly at crimes in which he had had a hand, and at crimes which he would yet commit when the opportunity arrived. Whenever a murder was committed, the doctor was the friend and advocate of the murderer, and vowed fierce vengeance against the judge and jury who condemned him to be hanged. When news of war and disaster came, he rubbed his hands, and gloated over it with glee, because he had prophesied what would happen through the imbecility and treason of infamous scoundrels who called themselves statesmen and generals.

From a Mutual Admiration Society, we became a society of iconoclasts. Tom, and Jack, and Sam, and Harry, and the rest of us, who had begun by swearing eternal friendship, were now bitter disputants, despising each other's mental qualities, calling each other duffers behind each other's backs, and laughing all the old modest pretensions to scorn. The loving-cups had faded out of memory. I passed the shop of our Benvenuto Cellini, the pewterer, one day, and saw the whole six exposed in the window for sale. I called upon Tom, to show him an article demolishing a popular author whom we had once idolized, and I noticed his loving-cup stowed away under the table with a waste-paper basket and a spittoon. It had grown dull and battered like a public-house pot, and was filled with short black pipes, and matches, and ends of cigars, and rubbish. I kicked it playfully with my foot, and laughed; and Tom blushed, and put it away out of sight.

Our society, in its new form, prospered exceedingly. We became famous for the freedom of our speech and the audacity of our opinions. Our company was much sought after, and we were proud of our originality and independence. We spent all our leisure hours together, and our defiant discussions kept us in a constant state of mental intoxication. But a sober moment arrived.

Tom and I sat together, one gloomy day, alone. We were solemn and moody, and smoked in silence. At length Tom said:

"Ned, I passed the shop to-day, and saw those six loving-cups in the window."

I replied, fretfully, "Bother the loving-cups!"

"No," said Tom, "I have other thoughts at this present moment; I have had them often, but have smothered them—smothered them ruthlessly, Ned; but they have always come to life again. They are very lively to-night—owing, perhaps, to the fog, or the state of my liver, or the state of my conscience—and I can't smother them."

"What do you mean, Tom?"

"You remember when we ordered the cups?"

"Yes."

"The doctor came among us shortly afterwards."

"He did."

"And we didn't carry out our intention."

"No. You paid for yours, Tom, and brought it away, but the rest are still unredeemed pledges of affection."

"Exactly," said Tom; "and that was owing to the doctor. He laughed at us. He made us ashamed of ourselves. He made me ashamed of myself. But I had paid for my cup, and brought it away, and the thing was done. If I had not done it when I did, I should never have done it. What were we ashamed of?"

"Silliness," I said.

"No, kindliness and good feeling, which we can't have too much of in this short journey."

I did not answer. Tom went on.

"This doctor has upset us all. He has changed our nature. He has turned the milk of human kindness that was in us, sour. He is a very fascinating person, I grant; but who is he? None of us know. He came among us mysteriously; we accepted him without question. Yet we don't know anything about him. We don't know what he is; what he does; where he lives; or even what country he belongs to."

"Well?"

"Well, I sometimes think he is the devil. He is very pleasant, but he is diabolical in all his views and opinions, nevertheless. If he is not the devil, he has, at any rate, played the devil with *us*. I feel it at quiet moments like these, when we are not excited and bandying flippant jokes and unbelieving sarcasms."

I smoked for a few moments in silence, and I then said:

"I feel it, too, exactly as you do, Tom. I have wished to say so often, only—only I didn't like."

"Ned, that is exactly what I have felt. Suppose we take courage now."

"Suppose we do," I said.

"Very well, then," said Tom. "Let us find out who this Doctor Goliath is, what he is, and all about him."

Tom had scarcely said the words when the doctor came in. He had a small bag in his hand, and a parcel under his arm.

"I am not going to stay this evening," he said. "I have work to do—work that the world will hear of. Ha!" And he contracted his brows darkly, and laid his finger on his nose in a portentous manner.

"Good night," he said; "if I survive, well and good; if not, remember me—but as to that, I don't imagine for a moment that you will do anything of the sort. You will say 'poor wretch,' and then go on with your jokes and your sport.

'Tis the way of this vile world, which has been a huge mistake from the beginning. Farewell."

"Ned," said Tom, "let us follow him."

We did so. We followed him into the Strand and on to the bridge, where he had an altercation with the toll-keeper. We could hear the words "swindle," "imposition," "highway robbery;" and we saw the doctor's face under the lamp glaring savagely at the man. At length he flung down his halfpenny, and walked hurriedly on, but stopped abruptly at the first recess, turned into it, and looked over the parapet at the river. We had long seriously entertained the suspicion—among many others of a like kind—that the doctor knew something about the mysterious, and as yet undiscovered, murder, which is associated with that spot. He had hinted at it himself often.

"Look!" said Tom. "Fascination draws him to the scene of his crime.—I almost wish he would throw himself over."

But the doctor did no such thing. After looking down at the river for a few moments, he leaped off the stone ledge, and passed on. We followed at a safe distance, and kept him in sight through a great many narrow and gloomy streets, where our only guide was the dark figure moving like a shadow before us. At length the doctor turned up a narrow passage, and disappeared.

We ran forward to the entrance, but the passage was completely dark, and we could see nothing. We hesitated for a moment, but immediately summoned up courage and followed, groping our way in the dark with the assistance of the wall. On coming out at the other end of this dark tunnel, we found ourselves in a triangular court lighted by a single gas-lamp placed at the apex of the triangle. There seemed to be no entrance to it save by the narrow passage through which we had passed.

All these strange and mysterious characteristics of the place we were enabled to see at a glance, by the aid of the one gas-lamp that stood like a mark of admiration in the corner. And that glance took in the cloudy figure of the doctor standing at a door in the darkest nook of the court, knocking. He was admitted before we reached the spot, but we had marked the house. It was number thirteen.

"An ogglesome number," said Tom. And there was an ogglesome plaster head over the doorway—a head, with a leer upon its face, and a reckoning-up expression, just like the doctor's. It seemed to be laughing at the fool's errand we had come upon.

I said, "What are we to do now?"

"Well, really, I don't know," said Tom.

"Stop," I cried; "I see a bill in the window. What does it say?"

Tom suggested, "Mangling done," as being most appropriate to a house inhabited by Doctor Goliath.

But it was not mangling. It was "Lodgings to let for a Single Gentleman."

"Let us knock," I said, "and inquire about the lodgings, and ascertain what sort of a place it is."

We saw a light pass into the first floor. That was evidently the doctor's room, and he had gone up-stairs. We waited a little, and then knocked. The door was opened by an elderly lady of exceedingly benignant aspect, who wore the remnants of a smile upon her face. The smile was evidently not intended for us, but we took it as if it were, and reciprocated with a smiling inquiry about the lodgings. Would we step in and look at them? They were two rooms down-stairs: a sitting-room and a bed-room. As the elderly lady, with a candle in her hand, was leading the way along the passage, the doctor called from above,

"Mrs Mavor, I want you here directly."

"Excuse me a moment, gentlemen," said Mrs Mavor; "the doctor, my first-floor lodger, has just come in, and wants his coffee. Pray take a seat in the parlour."

Mrs Mavor left us, and went up-stairs, and the next moment we heard the doctor saying in loud and angry tones:

"Where is my spider? How dare you sweep away my spider with your murderous broom?"

"Oh, the nasty thing!" we heard Mrs Mavor begin to say, but the doctor would not let her speak.

"Nasty thing! That's *your* opinion. What do you suppose that spider's opinion is of *you*, when you come and bring his house about his ears in the midst of his industry? How would you like it? Let me tell you that spider had as much right to live as you have; more—more! He was industrious, which you are not; he had a large family to support, which you have not; and if he did spread a net to catch the flies, don't you hang up 'Lodgings to Let,' and take in single young men like myself, and *do* for them? You are a heartless, wicked woman, Mrs Mavor."

Mrs Mavor came down almost immediately, laughing.

"That's my first-floor lodger, Doctor Goliath," she said; "he has strange ways in some things, and pretends to get in an awful temper if any one touches his pets; but he is such a good kind soul!"

Tom and I began to stare.

"He has been with me now over seven years," Mrs Mavor continued, "and he has behaved so well to me, and has been so kind to me when I have been ill, that nothing should induce me to take any person into the house that might disturb him or put him out of his ways. If the doctor were to leave Povis-place, I am sure I don't know what all the neighbours and the poor people about here would do; for he doctors them when they are ill, and he advises them when they are well, and he writes letters for them, and gets up subscriptions for them when there's any misfortune; and the children—they're all wild after him! Very often you'll see him here in the place, when he has been the gentlest and best of friends to their fathers and mothers, playing games with them, and a score of romping boys and girls on the top of his back—but *he* don't mind; he's so good-natured, and so fond of children!"

Tom and I were opening our eyes wider and wider. The doctor called again: "Mrs Mavor, bring me a ball of worsted, and let it be nice and soft."

Mrs Mavor went up-stairs with the worsted, and came back smiling.

"He has got his dumb pets round him now," she said, "and one of them has had an accident, and he can't bear to see the poor creature suffer. He is so tender-hearted!"

Tom and I were speechless. The doctor's pets, what could they be? Imps?

I said to Mrs Mavor, that we had heard of Doctor Goliath, that he was a very learned and skilful man, and that we would like to have a peep at him, if she would permit us. Mrs Mavor hesitated. He would be angry, she said, if he knew it. We put it upon our admiration for the man, and she consented; but we were only to peep through the door, and were not to make a noise.

We went up-stairs quietly to the doctor's landing. His door was ajar, and we could see nearly half the room through the crack, without being seen. If it had been possible to open our eyes any wider, we should have done it now.

For, the doctor was seated at a table on which his tea-things were laid. A canary-bird sat perched upon his head, a kitten was sporting at his feet, and he himself was occupied in binding up the leg of a guinea-pig.

"Poor little thing!" he was saying. "I am so sorry, so sorry; but never mind. There, there! I will bind up its poor little leg, and it will get well and run about as nicely as ever. Ah, little cat; now you know what I told you about that canary-bird. If you kill that canary-bird, I shall kill you. That is the law of Moses, little cat: it is a cruel law, I think, but I am afraid I should have to put it in force; for I love that little bird, and I love you, too, little cat, so you will not kill my pretty canary, will you? Sweet, sweet!" And the bird, perched upon the doctor's head, was answering "Sweet, sweet!"

Mrs Mavor was behind us, calling to us in a loud whisper to come away. We astonished Mrs Mavor and her lodger both. We walked right into the doctor's room.

He started at the sound of our footsteps; and when he saw us he turned pale with anger.

"What means this—this unwarrantable—this impertinent intrusion?"

He poured such a volley of angry words upon us that we were confused, and scarcely knew how to act. I saw that the only course was to take the bull by the horns.

"Doctor," I said, "you are an old humbug."

"What do you mean; what do you mean, sir? How dare you!" returned the doctor.

"And I say so too," stuck in the mild Tom, who had never before been known to speak so bold; "doctor, you are an old humbug."

"Well, upon my word," said the doctor, "the audacity of this proceeding—"

"Who taught us to be audacious, doctor?" Tom asked before he could finish the sentence.

The doctor gave way. He laughed, and he looked sheepish—as sheepish as we had looked when he discovered our loving-cup scheme. He scarcely knew what to say, and he put on a fierce look again, and called Mrs Mavor.

"How dare you allow strangers to enter my room in this manner? Take that bird and that mischievous cat and that nasty guinea-pig away, directly."

"It's of no use, doctor," said Tom; "we have found you out, and you can't deceive us any more. I have thought until now that you were an incarnate fiend, but I find you belong to the other side." Tom evidently meant that the doctor was a sort of angel, but he did not use the word; being probably struck with the incongruity of associating an angelic embodiment with a wide-awake hat and Blucher boots.

The doctor laughed: which encouraged Tom to address a moral lesson, on the doctor's conduct, to Mrs Mavor.

"To all of us, Mrs Mavor, he has made himself out a diabolical person: fierce, blood-thirsty, cruel. We had made a little Paradise among ourselves, and he entered it, like the beguiling serpent, and made us all wicked and unhappy. What did he do it for?"

Mrs Mavor, seeing that the doctor was getting the worst of it, plucked up courage and spoke out. "He does it everywhere beyond the boundaries of Povis-place, and I'll tell you what he does it for. *He is ashamed of being good, and kind, and tender-hearted!*"

"A pretty thing to be ashamed of," said Tom. "I've half a mind to punch his head!"

"No, don't," said the doctor, laughing. "Sit down and have a cup of coffee, and then Mrs Mavor will come and join us in a game of whist, and we'll have a potato-salad for supper, and I'll brew such a bowl of punch as I flatter myself no man on the face of the earth besides myself—"

"Doctor," said Tom again, "you're a humbug."

We told all to the society, and the next time the doctor came among us at Mrs Lirriper's here, he was received with shouts of derisive welcome.

The doctor gave a party in Povis-place, and we were all invited. There was so much victuals, there were so many bottles of German wine, and there was so large a number of guests, that Mrs Mavor's small tenement was in some danger of bursting. If I remember rightly, the provisions were on the scale of a ham and two fowls and a dozen of hocheimer, to each guest: to say nothing of the potato-salad, which was made in a bran new wash-hand basin, purchased for the occasion.

And after supper there was a presentation. The loving-cups had been redeemed; and one more was added to the number; and there they were, all bright and glittering—having been rubbed up expressly for the occasion—in a row upon the table. And the extra one was inscribed, "To the Doctor, from Tom, Ned, Sam, Will, Jack, Charley, and Harry, a Token of Friendship and Esteem."

Though our old heroes and idols are all set up on their pedestals long ago, Major, we are still given to cynical and audacious talk in our society, which is still held in my rooms here. But it deceives no one; and when the doctor tries to be fierce, he blushes at the feeble and foolish attempt he is making to conceal the tenderness of the kindest heart that ever beat.

THE BATTLE OF THE BARRELS.

The world will soon not be worth living in. Philanthropists, reformers, legislators, and social regenerators, are at work, day and night, rooting up, putting down, and sweeping away all the joys which make existence in this sublunary planet tolerable. At one time, if your donkey wouldn't go, you were at liberty to wallop him to the bare bone. You mustn't now. If you do, there is a Society down upon you. It's my belief that the present race of donkeys are aware of this; and that's what makes them so obstinate. The very cats are grown contumacious, and don't care how much row they kick up on the tiles; for they know that you musn't take them out and flay them alive in the back yard. They belong to the Society too; so do your wife and your dog. You musn't beat either, though it may be a pleasure to both parties. What *is* a man to beat? Upon my word, I don't know anything that is not in the Act of Parliament except the bounds of the parish, and they are a treat fit only for the workhouse.

You mustn't fight either. No; the practice of the noble art of self-defence without the gloves, is a breach of the peace. The French polishers of society forget the grand maxim: "If you wish for peace, prepare for war." How can you prepare for war if you are not allowed to practise the noble art of self-defence? You mustn't let your dog fight; though Dr Watts, an eminent divine, who was good, and wrote hymns, says, "It is his nature to." I tell you your laws are unnatural. There's nothing that game cocks like better than fighting with steel spurs on their heels. You say it is cruel. I tell you the cocks like it, revel in it. *I* like it. I revel in it. Why should you deprive me and my game cocks of our pleasure? Because you are determined to root all pleasure out of the earth, and make the world a howling wilderness. I would go out of the dull slow place altogether, but you won't even let me do that. If I throw myself over the bridge, and seek relief from the boredom of an intolerable existence in a watery grave, there is another Society at hand to run an iron hook into me, and bring me back to life and misery. It's these Societies that do all the mischief. The secretaries and officers must do something to earn their salaries. It's salaries that they're started for. I shouldn't be surprised if we were to hear next of a society for doing away with the sun. I dare say the gas companies would consider that the sun is a very improper thing, and ought to be put down.

It is surely and certainly coming to this when Parliament is actually talking of putting down the barrel-organs. Yes; the savage breast of this gloomy age is insensible to the charms of music. What does Mr Pope, who was a poet, say?

> Descend, ye Nine! descend and sing,
> The breathing instruments inspire!
> Wake into voice each silent string,
> And sweep the sounding lyre.

But what does Mr Bass, who is a brewer, say? Why, he says, "Take the Nine up, and lock them in the station-house." This is the difference between an age of poetry and barrel-organs, and an age of bitter ale and beer-barrels.

I am fond of music myself, and I am a friend of liberty, and oppressed and picturesque peoples. When I picture those poor but honest Savoyards, countrymen of Alfieri and Dante, leaving the sunny plains of fair Italy, bidding farewell to the fruitful fig-tree and the clustering vine, forsaking country, home, and friends, to go forth as missionaries of the divine art of music to the cold and inhospitable shores of the sunless north—when I call up this vision of heroic devotion in my mind's eye, and see Guiseppe and Giovanni scaling the Alpine heights in very indifferent shoes, but with fervour in their eyes and "Excelsior" on their banners, I am moved to the deepest sympathy and admiration. Welcome Guiseppe, welcome Giovanni! Welcome to England and Saffron-hill! He who does not love the organ-man has no bowels for humanity, no taste for music, no soul for poetry. The man himself is a man and a brother; and as to his instrument, what sings the poet, the same who bade the Nine descend?

> When the full organ joins the tuneful quire,
> Th' immortal powers incline their ear,
> Borne on the swelling notes our souls aspire,
> While solemn airs improve the sacred fire,
> And angels lean from Heaven to hear.

Yet there *are* people in the world who would put down the organs, who would hand over the discoursers of sweet music to the tender mercies of rude and ruthless policemen, fellows with souls for nothing but cook-maids, and tastes for nothing but cold mutton. In view of the immortal powers inclining their ears, and the angels leaning out of the windows of Heaven to hear, I can only say,

> The gods have pity where mankind have none.

If you are going to put down everything and do away with everything in this way, I want to know what a gentleman of independent property like myself is to do? How am I to be amused during the long hours of the day when there is nothing doing in the Haymarket? As I said before, you have left me nothing to be at; you won't let me aid and abet a fight; you forbid me to match my dog or my game cocks; and now you are going to deprive me of my barrel-organ, that sweet box of tunes, which comes, as I lie on the sofa smoking my cigar, to soothe me with Il Balen, and The Young Man from the Country, and the Dark Girl dressed in Blue. Oh, how I love that dark girl dressed in blue! I have never seen her, but music has painted all her charms, and I know that she is a smart young girl, a tall young girl, a nice young girl, and a dark young girl. All this in a flowing blue skirt. What a picture! It ravishes my soul! I send out a shilling to poor Giovanni, and bid him play it over again and again.

There are two lady patronesses of Giovanni's a few doors down on the other side of the way. Charming girls they are, with pink cheeks and frizzy hair, and nearly always sitting out in the balcony in low dresses. I fancy they are orphans, poor things, for I never see any one at the window who looks like a parent. They are passionately fond of music, and keep the organ-men playing to them for hours, and always pay them well; for I am happy to say that, though orphans, they appear to be well off, and go out in a Brougham.

There is another ardent lover of music at number one, an old gentleman who had a fortune left him on condition that he drove out every day in a coach-and-four. He has an organ to play to him at all his meals, and when the painter fellow, at number two, runs out with a maulstick in his hand to drive the musician away, the old gentleman has him into the garden, and makes him play there. There is another cantankerous man near me, who is always rushing out at the poor fellows and setting the police upon them. I don't know who he is; but he sits at a window all day long writing, and appears to work for his living. A pretty thing! if independent persons like myself and the old gentleman, and the two pretty ladies, are to be deprived of our pleasure to suit the whims and fancies of mere work-people.

The conceit of the fellows who "study," as they call it, is perfectly ridiculous. They think that the world cannot go on without them; that what *they* do is everything, and that everybody else ought to be hustled down and silenced. Just listen to Mr Babbage, who calls himself a philosopher;* "During the last ten years the amount of street music has so greatly increased, that it is now become a positive nuisance to a very consi-

* A Chapter on Street Nuisances, by Charles Babbage, Esq.

derable portion of the inhabitants of London. It robs the industrious man of his time; it annoys the musical man by its intolerable badness; it irritates the invalid, deprives the patient, who at great inconvenience has visited London for the best medical advice, of that repose which, under such circumstances, is essential to his recovery, and it destroys the time and the energies of all the intellectual classes of society by its continual interruptions of their pursuits."

This is rather a sweeping charge; let us see how he proves it. The instruments of torture—torture, indeed!—permitted by the government to be in daily and nightly use in the streets of London are thus enumerated: organs, brass bands, fiddles, harps, harpsichords, hurdy-gurdies, flageolets, drums, bagpipes—the delightful soul-inspiring bagpipes!—accordions, halfpenny whistles, tomtoms, trumpets, and the human voice divine, shouting out objects for sale, and in religious canting, and psalm-singing. The encouragers of street music are tavern-keepers, public-houses, gin-shops, beer-shops, coffee-shops, servants, children, visitors from the country, ladies of doubtful virtue, and occasionally titled ladies; but these are almost invariably of recent elevation, and deficient in that taste which their sex usually possess. And what does Mr Bass say to this? "The habit of frequenting public-houses and the amount of intoxication is much augmented by these means. It therefore finds support from the whole body of licensed victuallers, and from all those who are interested as the proprietors of public-houses."

Considering that Mr Babbage is a commander of the Italian order of St Maurice and St Lazarus, one might expect him to have some charity for the poor organ-grinder who comes from the same country as his decoration; but he has none. He is proud of the order of the dead beggar; but he has no bowels of compassion for the living one. His path is beset by him go where he will. On one occasion he fled from his tormentors to Cornwall, and there, within a few miles of the Land's End, he met one of the fellows whom he had frequently sent away from his own street. Some of Mr Babbage's neighbours have derived great pleasure from inviting musicians of various tastes and countries to play opposite his house, with the view of ascertaining whether there are not some kinds of instruments which he might approve; but their best efforts have had no other effect than to bring the philosopher out into the street in search of a policeman.

What a misfortune it is to a man to have no taste for music! There goes Mr Babbage in search of an officer of the law followed by a crowd of young children, urged on by their parents, and backed at a judicious distance by a set of vagabonds shouting forth uncomplimentary epithets, and making ridiculous rhymes on his name. When he turns round to survey his illustrious tail, it stops; if he moves towards it, it recedes; but, the instant he turns, the shouting and the abuse are resumed. In one case there were above a hundred persons, consisting of men, women, and boys, who followed him through the streets before he could find a policeman.

One day two fellows called "Stop thief!" after him, and then ran away. A foolish young fellow purchased a wind instrument with a hole in it, with which he made discordant noises for the purpose of annoying him. A workman inhabiting an attic which overlooked his garden, blew a penny whistle out of his window every day for half an hour. When Mr Babbage took measures to put a stop to these proceedings he was threatened with vengeance. One correspondent kindly volunteered to do him a serious bodily injury, while a third, in a personal communication, intimated his intention of burning the house down with Mr Babbage in it. The smaller evils of dead cats thrown down his area, of windows from time to time purposely broken, or of occasional blows on the head from stones projected by unseen hands, Mr Babbage will not condescend to speak of. All these things are trifles compared to being awakened at one o'clock in the morning (just as he has fallen asleep after a painful surgical operation) by the crash of a brass band. On a careful retrospect of the last dozen years of his life, Mr Babbage arrives at the conclusion that one-fourth part of his working power has been destroyed by street music—which he regards as a twenty-five per cent income-tax on his brain, levied by permission of the government, and squandered among the most worthless classes. During eighty days he registered one hundred and sixty-five instances when he went out to put a stop to the nuisance. In several of these instances his whole day's work was lost, for they frequently occurred when he was giving instructions to his workmen relative to some parts of his analytical engine.

This is the case of the workers. Let us now hear what Mr Babbage has to say on behalf of the invalids. It has been found by the returns of benefit societies that in London 4·72 persons in every hundred are constantly ill, which is equal to forty-seven in every thousand. In Mr Babbage's district the number of persons in a house averages ten. In Manchester-street, which faces his own residence, there are fifty-six houses. This, allowing the average stated, shows that about twenty-six persons are usually ill in that one street; but there are streets adjoining, to portions of which the music penetrates, so that if the portions of these streets are considered to be only equal in population to that of Manchester-street, we have upwards of fifty sick people, who are constantly disturbed by music.

These people, then, these slavish workers and obstinate invalids, claim protection. They demand that employment and ill-health shall be just and reasonable causes for forcing street musicians, not simply to move on, but to clear out of the neighbourhood altogether. They ask that the police, on any complaint whatever from an inhabitant, shall have no discretion, but shall be obliged to take the musician into custody and lock him up. This is all very well for the workers and the invalids, but what is to become of me, a gentleman of good health and independent property, who has no occasion to work, and who only wants to be amused? What is to become of the old gentleman at number one, who likes music at his dinner, when he comes from a drive in his coach-and-four? What is to become of the two young ladies with pink cheeks and frizzy hair? Labour has its duties no doubt; but property has its rights. What is Mr Babbage's calculating machine to me? I have five hundred a-year independent of the world, and when I go to the bank to receive my dividends, I can count the notes without a machine. The machine I require is an organ to play to me when I am dull, and want to kill time. What's the use of being independent if you can't enjoy yourself? One might just as well have to work.

Mr Bass, too, to head the crusade! It is just one barrel against another. But take heart, my poor, persecuted, ill-used, unappreciated Italians: Mr Gladstone is going to give us universal suffrage. You will have votes, you will return members to Parliament, you will bring in a bill to put down beer-barrels, and you will have your revenge.

DEBT.

The greatest curse of this land is not, as some imagine, drink, but debt. There are many persons in a position to declare that, among all their acquaintances, they do not know a drunkard. I believe, however, there is not one who does not know several persons who are in debt, and who suffer great misery in consequence. In whatever rank of society you move, from the very highest down to the very lowest, you cannot live long without becoming acquainted with men and women who are a trouble to themselves, and to their friends, through owing money. So completely does insolvency pervade society, that those who are not in debt are almost as much victims to the consequences as those who are. What does it avail me that I pay on the nail for everything, and owe no man anything, when I have relatives, and friends, and acquaintances who are in debt to every one with whom they deal? They come and carry off the money I have saved by my prudence and economy; they come and vex my heart with distresses, which, in my own case, I have taken infinite pains to avoid. They make their debts my debts, and their troubles my troubles. I might almost as well have incurred debt and trouble for myself.

I have lost all patience with these people, and I intend now to read them a lecture. I trust it may do them good.

To begin with, then: The great majority of them are persons who have no business to be in debt at all. I make no doubt whatever that the credit system is essential to the conduct of wholesale business, that the great commercial machine could not get on without it. But I am sure that its extension to the minor dealings of society is the source of a vast amount of misery and wretchedness, that can in no way be attributed to the freaks of fortune, or the chances of life.

There are many excuses for the failure of a merchant, liable to the fluctuations and losses incidental to trade; there is every excuse for the insolvency of a man with an inadequate salary, and an intolerably large family. But there is no excuse whatever for the thousands of middle-class people, with fixed incomes of considerable amount, who are constantly in debt and difficulty, and who only manage to scramble through life by making compromises with their creditors, by "going through the court," or by evading their liabilities altogether. It is among this moderately well-to-do middle class that the greatest amount of embarrassment is to be found, and it mainly arises from the indolent and thoughtless habit—for it is nothing but a habit—of obtaining goods upon credit.

It may be laid down as a principle, that the man who takes credit and the man who gives it both place themselves at a disadvantage. You are in debt to your butcher, and, as a consequence, the butcher is in debt to the salesman. The butcher sues you and the salesman sues the butcher. You are both in a mess, both unhappy. A ready-money transaction would have saved both of you. The butcher would have got more for his money, and so would you. Every one who is accustomed to pay on the nail is aware that he gets his goods considerably cheaper than those who take credit. A loaf of bread bought and paid for at the counter costs, say sixpence-halfpenny. If it be put down in the book it is charged a penny or twopence more. Ready money also commands a choice, and full weight, which credit does not. There is, perhaps, no great choice in loaves; but there is great variety in sirloins of beef and legs of mutton.

If you run a bill with a butcher he sends you what he likes, charges you smartly for credit, and possibly takes advantage of you in the matter of weight. Perhaps you are a very genteel person, and consider it beneath your dignity to go about to butchers and bakers chaffering for joints of meat and loaves of bread. Well; if your income be over three hundred a year, you are possibly in a position to indulge your gentility; but if it be anything under that amount, you cannot afford to be genteel at so heavy a cost. Every income, whatever may be its amount, requires careful management. It is just as easy to get into debt and difficulty with a few thousands a year as with a few hundreds. Perhaps the safest position is that of the man who earns two or three pounds a week. His income is so small that no one will trust him, and so he is obliged to buy his goods as he wants them, and pay for them with ready money. This person cannot live genteelly, but by management he gets enough to eat and drink, and is never troubled with duns and creditors. By avoiding credit, a man may live and support a family upon a hundred a year without getting into debt. By taking credit, he will be in debt with ten thousand a year.

It is a very simple matter. Credit never permits a man to know the real value of money, nor to have full control over his affairs. It presents all his expenses in the aggregate, and not in detail. Every one has more or less of the miser's love of money—of the actual gold pieces and the crisp bank-notes. Now, if you have these things in your pocket, you see them, as you make your purchases, visibly diminishing under your eyes. The lessening heap cries to you to stop. You would like to buy this, that, and the other; but you know exactly how much money you have left, and that if you go on buying more things your purse will soon be empty. You do not see this when you take credit. You give your orders freely, without thought or calculation; and when the day of payment comes, you find that you have overrun the constable.

The honest and the dishonest, the careful and the reckless, all fall victims to this snare. They begin life by owing, and they never know what it is to have direct control over their means. The consequence is, that they are utterly without a guide to the scale by which they ought to live. People who owe instead of paying for what they require, invariably pitch that scale too high. Let us take the case of a man with three hundred a year. Being a gentleman born and bred, and married to a lady, he considers it necessary that he should have a genteel house. Now, in London you cannot get a house with any pretensions to gentility for less than sixty pounds a year. Well, perhaps a man with three hundred a year can afford to pay sixty pounds for his house. But how seldom does he reckon that the actual sum he will have to pay, including rates and taxes, is close upon eighty pounds?

Then comes the furnishing. The young man, seeing that other persons with the same means as himself have well-appointed houses, at once proceeds to furnish his residence from kitchen to attic, on credit. I say on credit, for if he were possessed of the necessary money, he would wait and furnish it by degrees. He now commences life as a householder, keeps a cook and a housemaid, runs bills with all his tradespeople, maintains a genteel establishment, gives little parties, and lives happily—for three months. At the end of that time bills tumble in upon him, and he finds that their united amount is considerably more than his quarter's salary. If his creditors press him, he is driven to borrow money at ruinous interest; and so he is fairly launched upon a career of misery. And all for the want of the commonest prudence.

Three hundred a year is a salary upon which a family may live comfortably; but not luxuriously. It will not admit of ad-libitum expenditure; it must be nursed, and managed, and watched. A man with this amount of salary ought not to pay more than sixty pounds a year for house rent, including taxes, and he ought to purchase his furniture by degrees. He has no business to set up as a full-blown householder in a moment. If he can manage to complete his furnishing in two or three years, he will do very well. In any case he cannot afford to pay a premium of five-and-twenty or thirty per cent on every stick he buys. On the contrary, it is necessary that he should get everything at the very cheapest. This is only to be done by paying ready money, and ready money is only to be got by living for a year or two within one's income.

Everything in nature grows by degrees—everything but the human donkey, which tries to be a magnificent animal, as like a lion as possible, in a minute. Let me enumerate a few things which a man cannot afford to do with an income of no more than three hundred a year. He cannot afford two servants; he cannot afford to give set parties; he cannot afford three courses and a dessert every day; and, as a broad rule, he cannot afford to take three months' credit from his tradespeople. Two servants will cost him at the very least sixty pounds a year, an amount entirely out of proportion to his means. Then that three course and a dessert business is the very type of a mockery, a delusion, and a snare.

It may be said that a plate of soup does not cost much; that a bit of fish is an inexpensive luxury; that a pudding is a very simple viand. That, perhaps, is true, of each of these dishes separately; but collectively, as forming the daily bill of fare in a small establishment, they will be found to come very costly. At an eating-house you can get a basin of soup for a shilling, or a plate of salmon or turbot for the same amount. But you cannot make a shilling's worth of soup at home; you cannot buy a shilling's worth of salmon. A dinner of this kind cooked for two persons will cost at the very least three shillings a head. Six shillings a day for dinners, to say nothing of the consumption and waste below-stairs, on a salary of less than a pound a day! No; clearly this will not do. The stern fact must be faced; there must be a good deal of plain but substantial boiled beef and roast mutton, occasionally cold, about the dinners in a three hundred a year establishment. Better is a dinner of herbs with love, than the stalled ox and contention therewith. Better cold mutton and pickles now and then with independence, than three courses and dessert with duns besieging your gate. People do not really care about these dinners. When Paterfamilias is in the City he will dine off a chop, and be satisfied; but at home he must do the grand. It is a mere habit with some; with others it is ostentation and pretence. Besides, life is not all for meat and drink. Banyan days are good for the health; the occasional fast gives zest to the periodical feast.

Parties are madness. More people are ruined by parties than by anything else. A three hundred a year establishment cannot afford to call in the confectioner more than once a year. Indeed, I doubt if it can bear up against that expensive administrator at all. If you have a grand party of this kind, with an ornamental supper, and wine and waiters, you cannot do much less than the man who counts his income by thousands. Your guests eat and drink as much as his guests, and you cannot offer them cheap pheasants and cheap champagne. The great error which people with small incomes commit, is in thinking that they are bound to do the same as their friends and neighbours.

What nonsense this is! Smith and Jones mix in society on the same footing because they are both gentlemen, but if Smith has a thousand a year and Jones three hundred, is it reasonable that Jones should be expected to give as grand parties as Smith? It is not reasonable. No one expects it; and when Jones gives his grand parties, the guests roll home in their carriages and speculate upon their host's speedy bankruptcy. But there is a kind of party-giving practised by humble folks, which, though very unpretending, is quite as expensive. You will hear modest householders say,

"Drop in any evening and smoke a pipe with me; I don't pretend to give wine, and that sort of thing, but I can offer you a bit of supper and a glass of grog."

Drop in any time, according to invitation, and you will find half a dozen fellows smoking pipes and drinking humble gin-and-water. But gin, though humble, costs money, and half a dozen fellows will drink a lot of it, and they generally stay to supper and drink more gin; and the humble party costs the host a pound at the very least. He can't afford it. He wouldn't do it if he had to put his hand in his pocket for the money every time a bottle of gin is wanted. But he takes credit, and has only to send for it. You think me a shabby fellow because I don't keep open house in the same fashion. Very well; have that opinion; but I promise you I will not get into debt and come and borrow money of you. Your liberal friend will, and you might as well pay him for his entertainment at the time. I don't say that a man ought not to give parties. Parties are very pleasant when everything is paid for, and you can afford to give them; but a man with three hundred a year can afford to entertain his friends only when he has the spare cash in his purse to defray the expense. It is bad enough to take credit for the necessaries of life; but to run a bill for champagne and trifle is an offence that merits whipping.

A select committee of noblemen's stewards assembled, not very long ago, to furnish estimates of the expense of keeping up a first-rate establishment in first-rate style. They all hit close to the same mark; one mentioned forty-two thousand, another forty-five, and another—this being the highest—forty-seven thousand. It was eventually agreed that a nobleman could live in first-rate style, keep his town and country houses, his horses and hounds, and entertain his friends magnificently, for forty-five thousand pounds a year, provided—there was a proviso even in this case—provided that the *income were carefully aud prudently managed.*

The stewards would not answer for the consequences if their masters went to work recklessly, spending right and left, and indulging their fancies without regard to the limit prescribed by their means. The truth is, that every income, whatever its amount, whether three hundred or forty-five thousand, requires to be managed with care and prudence. Everything is in degree. Tastes and habits advance with the amount of income, and the man who lives above his three hundred will find it just as easy to live above forty thousand. Extravagance can always find a way of indulging itself; recklessness will squander even millions. As a rule, however, noblemen with thousands a year are much more careful than the little people with a few hundreds. In many great houses there is a steward, or an accountant, who makes out the bills every month, and at regular intervals places a balance-sheet of assets and expenditure before his master.

This steward is very often a privileged person, who will not scruple to tell my lord and my lady that they are going too fast, that they must forego certain pleasures, live more quietly, and retrench. It is generally the small people who live without check or control. And among all the small people there is no more aggravating instance of extravagance and unthrift than that of the man who, with an income varying from eight hundred to a thousand a year, is always needy, always borrowing money, always involved with Jew bill-discounters and sheriffs' officers. The thousand a year people seem to be the most unfortunate of all: they are always in a mess. There must be something particularly awkward about the sum. Judging from all I have seen, it is both too little and too much. I imagine the case to be this:—when a man's income is under a thousand, he is content with a genteel house at sixty pounds a year and two or three female servants; when it reaches a thousand, he feels himself justified in taking a mansion and setting up a man-servant and a carriage.

Now, in London, a thousand a year won't bear this. It won't pay for the flash and show attendant upon livery servants and a carriage. As a rule, if a man with a thousand a year give outward indications in his dress and habits of being above the ordinary run of people you meet in the street, you may be sure he is overrunning the constable. A thousand a year, to be really comfortable and well off, must walk a good deal, ride a good deal on the top of the omnibus, and be content with champagne dinners and a box at the Opera as an occasional treat. It may be laid down as a rule, that a thousand a year cannot afford to pay more than a hundred a year for rent and taxes. In London there is no graduated scale of houses to suit incomes that vary only by a hundred or so. A thousand a year does not justify a better house than five hundred. There is nothing between the moderately genteel residence and the female servants, and the mansion involving a carriage and footmen.

It used to be said that fools built houses and wise men lived in them. But this was a proverb of our ancestors, who made haste gently in the matter of living. Now-a-days landlords and tenants are all fools together. Not long ago I observed the tax-gatherer proceeding on his rounds. I watched him through a whole street in a genteel region, and I am certain, by the momentary stay he made at each door, that he did not receive the taxes at a single house. I thought it extremely probable that the landlords had not received their rents.

The whole system is rotten to the core. On every hand we see people living on credit, putting off pay-day to the last, making in the end some desperate effort, either by begging or borrowing, to scrape the money together, and then struggling on again, with the canker of care eating at their hearts, to the inevitable goal of bankruptcy. If people would only make a push at the beginning instead of the end, they would save themselves all this misery. The great secret of being solvent, and well-to-do, and comfortable, is to get ahead of your expenses. Eat and drink this month what you earned last month: not what you are going to earn next month.

There are, no doubt, many persons so unfortunately situated that they can never accomplish this. No man can guard against ill health; no man can ensure himself a well-conducted helpful family, or a permanent income. There will always be people who cannot help their misfortunes. But, as a rule, these unfortunates are far less trouble to society than those in a better position who bring their misfortunes upon themselves by deliberate recklessness and extravagance. You may help a poor honest struggling man to some purpose. But the utmost you can do for an unthrift is thrown away. You give him money you have earned by hard labour and saved by self-denial and economy, and he spends it in pleasures which you have never permitted yourself to enjoy.

A measure is proposed by the Lord Chancellor, the direct object of which may be said to be—to make people thrifty by Act of Parliament. It is possible that it may have some effect in controlling the reckless practices of tradesmen, who, having no dread of the Court of Bankruptcy before their eyes, are ever anxious to force credit upon customers on the mere chance of payment; it may afford some protection to poor debtors against the ruthless operation of the law directed by unscrupulous and rapacious creditors; but it will never compel people to live within their means—that is to say, it will never teach common prudence and common honesty.

The great marvel is that so many people should deliberately choose to be miserable when they might just as easily be happy. It is the greatest mistake in the world to suppose that pleasure must be expensive. It is nothing of the kind. The best pleasures, those which sweeten life most, and leave no bitterness behind, are cheap pleasures. What greater pleasures can a man enjoy than the sense of being free and independent? The man with his fine house, his glittering carriage, and his rich banquets, for which he is in debt, is a slave, a prisoner, for ever dragging his chain behind him through all the grandeur of the false world in which he moves. I will go out this morning with the consciousness that I owe no man anything, that even the bright day is earned and paid for, and I will walk to Highgate, and, being weary, and hungry, and athirst, I will enter a wayside inn and feast upon bread and cheese, washing it down with a mug of ale, and there will be no pleasure superior to mine in all Christendom.

TURNING OVER A NEW LEAF.

NEW-YEARS' DAYS are the milestones on the journey of life. What a weary journey it would be without those milestones! The traveller over the waste of time would be like a mariner on a trackless sea without rudder or compass—a cast-away! Just imagine mankind without a calendar —seasons following seasons, and years gliding into years, without a resting-place from which to look back upon the past, and forward into the future. I do not know how we can realize this except upon some desert journey, where there are no landmarks to tell us how far we have travelled, and how many weary miles yet lie beyond. He who has travelled such a road can tell how long the miles appear, how heavily the time hangs, how weary become the feet! As you trudge onward, seeing nothing to give you assurance that you are nearing the goal, your heart sinks for want of hope. You do not know how far you have come; you cannot guess how far you have yet to go. Oh! for a stone or post to tell you that you have accomplished some definite portion of your journey, if it be only one single mile; for then you know the extent of your toil. At such landmarks you sit you down, as on an oasis, and bathe your wayworn feet, and dry your tears, and rise refreshed and strengthened for the next stage on your journey.

How infinite is the mercy of Heaven in adapting times and seasons to man's estate and condition! Let us suppose a sudden change, and that the earth occupied two years in revolving round the sun—that the four seasons were doubled in length. How the tedium of opening spring would provoke us! how the glory of summer would pall upon us! how the lingering promise of autumn would make the heart sick! and how terrible would be the dread of the coming winter! But to realize this more forcibly, let us imagine a day of forty-eight hours—twenty-four hours of day, and the same number of night. As it is, many of us talk of killing Time. But in such a case, would not all mankind be in league to put an end to him once and for ever? So intolerable does the bare idea of such an arrangement appear, that the order of things in the inhabited regions near the poles may almost be regarded as a defect in the Great Scheme. These regions are apt to give us the idea of outhouses attached to the Great Building, which were never intended to be inhabited except by reindeer and bears. Tell a fashionable cockney of a place where they never draw down the blinds and light the lamps for five months, and he will faint. Perhaps the seven months when the blinds are permanently drawn down, and the lamps are always burning, would suit him better; but he would get tired even of that. The fool's paradise of eternal night-revels would be a pandemonium. Nature has set us an example in the ordering of seasons, and the marking of time, which we have followed in our own small way by instituting minor subdivisions. It may be said, God made years and days, and man made hours and minutes and seconds. It is well that the plan has been thus artificially extended, for we stand in need of the most frequent reminders of the flight of time. Without these bells of warning, clashing for ever around us, the sands of life would steal away like a thief, robbing us of many wholesome seasons of thought and sober reflection.

But we take small note of these minor warnings. *Carpe diem* is a maxim little heeded. A miserly maxim. As if a day were of any account! A youth with many years in store for him throws away a day as a rich man throws away a guinea. "There are plenty more. The sun will rise to-morrow, and to-morrow, and to-morrow, and my purse will fill with days as fast as it is emptied."

Weeks! what do they mark but a brief period in our course of toil or pleasure? Months! Do we not sometimes forget whether it is August or September? Years! But here we pause. Days, weeks, months, may preach to us in vain, but years will make us hold and listen—especially when we have turned thirty. Before that age most young men are proud of the fact that they are growing older. They hear their seniors prate of their age and experience, and they envy age and experience as, at another period of their existence, they envied whiskers and tail-coats. But when thirty years are passed, and the figures are rapidly leading on to twoscore, a man becomes as unwilling—ay, as unwilling as any woman—to confess that he is as old as he really is. He would like to be thought younger—he would like *to be* younger.

This is about the time of life when men begin to exclaim

"Eheu fugaces anni labuntur!"

It has been but a line from Horace hitherto, something to scan, something to quote to show off your Latinity. But now it is a stern, inexorable voice, challenging you on the threshold of a new year. You have serious thoughts now; you are wise now—now that half of your threescore is gone. Why were you not serious, why were you not wise before, when you were one-and-twenty, entering upon manhood and life, ten years ago? "Fool, fool, fool! If I had had such thoughts then as I have now, what might I not have accomplished ere this?" Well, it is no use biting your lips, and stamping your foot. It is a true and wholesome proverb which says you cannot put an old head upon young shoulders. There is no fitness in the thing: man must have time to develop his head, as a cabbage must have time to develop its heart. I for one do not believe in William Pitt, prime minister at twenty-three. He might have been as learned as Bacon, but what could he have known of the philosophy of life? How could he have known that which he never saw? Solomon was not wise because he read books.

According to my experience of life, derived from observation, and the perusal with the keenest interest of many biographies, "thirty" is the golden number in the years of a man's life. This is the middle milestone upon which he rests to survey the past and contemplate the future. Woe to him who does not rest and think now! for at this time the mind is more candid and the heart more open to the touch of truth and tenderness than it ever will be again, until, perhaps, the day when there is no hope left. If you look around in your society, and mark the men who have passed the Rubicon of forty-five or fifty, still retaining health and strength, you will find that the *fugaces anni* trouble them little. Men at this age think less of death than youths of half their years. They seem to look upon the midway of their age as the crisis of a disease, and that when they have passed this bridge they have got over the worst. I remember, when I first began to think seriously of the fleeting years, asking a boisterous old gentleman if the thought of his narrowing span ever troubled him. I can recall our brief colloquy word for word.

"Ever trouble me! not in the least; not half so much as when I was your age."

"But," I said, "does it never occur to you that your time is getting very short, and that you must go some day soon?"

"Not at all," he said; "I am strong and hearty, and I feel to have just as good a prospect of life as ever I had. When I was twenty I thought I should die before I came of age. Now I am sixty-three. I see no reason why I shouldn't live to be a hundred."

I know my friend well, and I am not going to hold him up as an awful example, for that would be to mistake his case altogether. He is not a man hardened in sin, but a man hardened in years. He has got used to living, and thinks he will live on indefinitely just the same; as a man used to wealth thinks he will always have turtle and champagne for dinner. I don't say that this is not a comfortable state of feeling to arrive at, so as you carry with you a pure heart and a clear conscience; but I think you miss the lesson which chasteneth a man to most profit, and teacheth him most fully the philosophy of life, if you escape over the bridge of mid-life without passing through the valley of the shadow of serious thoughts.

Age does not alone blanch the hair and wrinkle the cheek. I will not say it hardens the heart, but it dulls the feelings and blunts the sensibilities. Neither very young nor very old people feel the loss of friends so keenly as do persons of middle age. The young are too buoyant of spirit to be deeply touched by grief: the old have stood by many graves. At thirty you feel the loss of friends and companions keenly. You set out with them on the journey, full of strength, and life, and hope; and now they have fallen by the wayside, one by one,—those you loved best perhaps,—and you are alone with strangers. There was a time when you could not have imagined life tolerable without those friends of your heart; but what have you done when they sank beside you on the road, but paused for a moment, and said, "Poor fellow!" dropping a single tear, and passing on. There is a bitter but profitable reflection in this. A man of great mark, much esteemed, and held in high regard by the circle in which he moves, sinks into an untimely grave. Just for the moment there is a hush among those who knew him; a few tears are shed, a few grave looks are interchanged; but to-morrow brings dry eyes and cheerful faces, and his friends eat and drink and make merry before the week is out.

The persons who do this are not more heartless than the rest of their kind. It is a failing common to humanity. It is hard to grieve enough. Often and often I have caught myself laughing and making merry when I felt that I had yet a heavy debt of tears to pay to a dead friend. So it will be with you. You will die, and the friends who now "grapple you to their souls with hooks of steel" will be gay of heart with the next sun. There are some who ridicule the conventional ensigns of grief, "the trappings and the suits of woe." They are wrong. It is the only way in which poor weak humanity can give permanence to its sorrow. Let us show it on our hats, if we cannot in our hearts, that we are grieving for a friend. Let crape redeem our cold stint of tears. I hold that the least we can do for a friend when he is dead is to pay all honour to his remains. When he is alive, do we not set our house in order to receive him; do we not place the choicest viands before him, and allot him our best room? Does he need all the superfluities which we press upon him? No. But we are lavish in our attentions that we may show him respect. And shall we have no further regard for him when the spirit has fled, and his clay—that clay which we honoured so much in the warmth of life—has grown cold? Away with your hard shopkeeping maxims! Leave me to pillow the head of my dead friend upon the softest satin, and furnish his last house with becoming state. It is the last service I can render him. I cannot pay him all the debt of grief I owe him. Let me wring my purse-strings if I cannot wring my heart-strings.

I am reminded of Queen Elizabeth's injunctions to the discursive preacher at Paul's Cross. "To your text, Mr Dean—to your text!"

Well, my text is "Turning over a new leaf," and I am coming to the point in my own way. This night, when the last days of the year are ebbing away, I have discovered a gray hair—the first gray hair! I had never seen such a thing—never dreamt of such a thing! At *my* age: I could not believe it.

It was laid upon a band of black velvet and placed before me.

I can resist conviction no longer. There it lies, blanched and white—white as the driven snow! And it is *my* hair. It seems but yesterday that I was at school, wishing I were a man. And now to-day I am gray, and growing old. What have I done in all this time? Have I fulfilled a man's mission upon earth—have I made any step towards it? Have I done any good in the most infinitesimal degree, for which the world is wiser or better? I cannot answer my own questions. I am dumb, and sitting here contemplating that white hair, with the sense that another year is gliding away, I feel that it is time in right good earnest to turn over a new leaf. I have made the resolution often before, but never under the sense of obligation which now weighs upon me.

I remember a certain "Hogmanay" night, ten years ago, when half a dozen young fellows sat round a certain hospitable fire, which has, alas! been quenched. We were not, any of us, in good heart, and we resolved with the new year to turn over a new leaf. It was a trifling proceeding—little better than sport. When twelve o'clock struck, one laid down his pipe, and said, 'From this moment I give up smoking;' another threw his box into the fire, and said, 'I will snuff no more;' a third said, 'I forswear billiards henceforward;' a fourth resolved to master the German language before that day twelve months. These were small leaves to turn over; but the result was not unimportant. These vows made in concert, at the midnight hour of the last night of the old year, were kept for twelve months. The smoker and the snuffer relapsed; but the billiard-player broke himself of a passion for play, and was a richer man for it. The aspiring linguist learnt German well enough to read it, and has been a man of more value in his vocation ever since. Would that I could meet all those friends again on the last day of this waning year, that we might resolve anew, and on a broader plan! I would say to them, "Let us begin the new year with chastened hearts, and with a resolve to shape all our actions by the rule of Christian charity; let us measure all we do by the gauge of truth, for then, whatever be the result, we shall have the consolation of knowing that we have striven to walk in the right path." But, alas! that same company will never meet together on earth again.

It is the fashion with many persons to dance the old year out, as if it were a matter for rejoicing that another period of life is gone. I hold it is no time for dancing nor for mirth. It is a time for thought and serious reflection; a moment to pause and gird up our loins for a fresh start on the journey of life. The time is peculiarly favourable for making new resolutions, and if they are solemnly made by a family, or social circle by the fireside, as the bells ring out the knell of the old year, they are more likely to be remembered and kept than if they were made at a less impressive moment.

Thirty years ago, a young man began to feel the burden of a rapidly increasing family. His companions in the race of life pitied him, and prophesied that he would never get on, with so large a family dragging upon him. The young man himself quailed before his responsibility, and almost lost heart, for he had already seven children, and was little more than thirty years of age. But on the last night of a certain year he made a resolution. He said, "I will do my duty by my children; I will strain every nerve to give them a good education to fit them for making their way in the world."

For this end he toiled and slaved, and denied himself; and when his friends and associates saw him in rusty clothes, and with careworn looks, plodding on year after year, getting poorer rather than richer, they sighed for his hard lot, through the *curse* of a large family that weighed upon him and crushed him.

That imagined curse became a blessing. That man is now in the sere and yellow leaf, happy, contented, and well provided for by his sons and daughters, who, through the superior education they received, are now occupying positions in life which may almost be termed brilliant. This is no parable.

I have preached my sermon, and have only to add one "lastly" to my congregation. Don't dance out the old year; don't let it slip away amid mirth and thoughtlessness. Seize the moment to be sober and thoughtful—to make good resolutions for the future. When these are made, with a strong heart, and a firm will, then may we truly wish each other a Happy New Year.

FRIENDS TILL DEATH.

There are some men whose lives might be written in a single page, so even has been the tenor of their career, so unchequered the course of their existence. Take for example old Gilliflower and his friend Bardsley. I knew Gilliflower and Bardsley when they first set up in business in Toocum Street; the one as a grocer and the other in the ironmongery line. They came into the street about the same time and opened shop next door to one another. They were not then personally acquainted; and like many other next-door neighbours in a large city, passed years in sight of each other without contracting any closer acquaintanceship than that of neighbourly civility. They would say "A fine day, sir," as they took down their shutters of a morning; or, "A fine evening, sir," as they put them up again at night. If these morning and evening civilities were varied, it was simply by a change of the adjective. Toocum Street being an English street, the variation was doubtless frequent.

But Gilliflower and Bardsley were destined to

become fast friends; indeed friends till death. There was nothing romantic in the way in which this friendship was contracted. It was not through Gilliflower's house catching fire, and Bardsley making superhuman efforts to rescue Gilliflower from the flames. Nor *vice versâ*. Nor did Bardsley plunge into any river after Gilliflower; nor did Gilliflower plunge in after Bardsley. It arose, I am bound to say, entirely out of a question of beer. Both shopkeepers were unmarried and without encumbrance.

When the labours of the day were over, Bardsley was wont to adjourn to the Green Dragon to smoke his pipe and drink his flagon of ale. Gilliflower patronized another house—the Boar. A great point in the character of both men was constancy, or what in politics would be called conservatism. A practice once adopted was never, or rarely, departed from. Once having established a corner in the parlour of the Green Dragon, Bardsley would as soon have thought of changing his wholesale dealer as of going to the Lion or the King's Head. Gilliflower, on his part, was as closely attached to his corner at the Boar.

It happened, however, some three or four years after his first visit to the Boar, that the landlord of that establishment was induced to change his brewer. Gilliflower was one of the first to be served with the new tap. He didn't like it. It might have been very good beer; it might have been better beer than that formerly supplied, but it was not the kind of beer he had been accustomed to. Gilliflower was a patient man, and bore it as long as he could; but there was a limit even to Gilliflower's patience; and with something of a pang at parting from his own corner and particular Windsor chair, the worthy grocer at length transferred his patronage to the Dragon. On his first visit to that establishment he found his neighbour Bardsley ensconced by the chimney-corner smoking his pipe.

"Good evening, sir," said Gilliflower.

"Good evening, sir," returned Bardsley.

"Coldish to-night, sir," said Gilliflower, taking a chair.

"Coldish indeed, sir," said Bardsley.

Here there was a pause of some duration. It was at length broken by Gilliflower ringing for the waiter.

"I think," said Gilliflower, half to himself and half to Bardsley, "I'll try a drop of their ale."

"You'll find it to your taste, sir, I think," said Bardsley.

The ale was placed on the table, flanked by a pipe and a paper of tobacco.

"Your good health, sir," said Gilliflower, eyeing the liquor knowingly.

"The same to you, sir," said Bardsley.

"Body there, sir?"

"And hops, sir?"

"And hops, sir."

Bardsley and Gilliflower puffed in silence for the next ten minutes. At length Bardsley said:

"Seasonable weather."

Gilliflower said, "Very seasonable."

Another long silence, broken only by puffs. Then Gilliflower:

"How do you find business, sir?"

"Well, I can't complain. How do you find it, sir?"

"Pretty tidyish, as things go; no reason to complain neither," said Gilliflower.

"Will you take a glass with me, sir?" said Bardsley.

"Well, thank you, sir, I will."

"Will you take a glass with me?" said Gilliflower by and by.

"Most happy, sir, I am sure," replied Bardsley.

That night as Gilliflower retired to his bachelor-couch he expressed (to himself) an opinion highly favourable of Bardsley. "A very agreeable man is that Bardsley—very agreeable man."

About the same moment Bardsley was tying

on his night-cap and saying, "An uncommon nice man that Gilliflower."

* * * * * *

Thirty years after it was said by Bardsley himself that he had never missed passing an evening in Gilliflower's company until that evening. But on that evening Gilliflower's chair was empty. The sight of it touched poor Bardsley's heart. The friend of his bosom was not there.

"And why?" said Bardsley to himself, as he gazed at the empty chair with misty eyes. "Because he is ill a-bed, and is not able to toddle so far." "Shall I sit here then," said Bardsley, "a-drinking and a-smoking and enjoying of myself while Gilliflower is ill a-bed?"

Bardsley answered the question by pushing away his pipe and pot with a reproachful air, and going to see his friend.

Thirty years had made Bardsley and Gilliflower fast friends. From the evening of their first meeting in the parlour of the Dragon, their attachment grew day by day, and increased with every pipe and pot until in feeling, in taste, and in habits they became as one man. Such was the identity of all spirituality in the two men, that the same body might have served for both. Knowing and reading those two minds, it might have occurred to an observer that nature had displayed a sad want of economy in making Bardsley and Gilliflower various. There was no corner of Bardsley's mind that was not known to Gilliflower, nor was there a cranny of Gilliflower's that was not revealed to Bardsley. Nor is this ascribing any great amount of acuteness to either party. Bardsley had taken as many bad shillings as any man, and Gilliflower's name was enrolled on the list of more than one begging letter-writer. It was not then the acuteness of Gilliflower's perception that discovered the profound depths of Bardsley's mind, but it was Bardsley's single and simple mind that displayed itself like a proclamation in large letters to Gilliflower's modest vision. And *vice versâ.* Innocence, honesty, kindliness of heart, and the most charming stupidity distinguished them both. They were just children who could smoke a pipe and drink a glass, and help each other on in the world, and sympathize with each other, without outgrowing either their clothes or their mutual attachment. In the first week of their acquaintance they had seen and known as much of each other as they ever saw and knew till death; because in that week all that was to be seen and known of both was fully laid open. And it was a very child's lesson all in the easiest words of one syllable. Business prospered moderately with both men. They had their struggles, as most people have. But Bardsley and Gilliflower were both won't to say, "I have always a friend." I may tell the reader, privately, that Bardsley's friend was Gilliflower, and that Gilliflower's friend was Bardsley. By a strange but happy coincidence, when Bardsley wanted ten pounds to make up a bill, Gilliflower always had it to lend him, and when Gilliflower wanted ten pounds Bardsley could always help Gilliflower. Fate had mortised their exigencies to a nicety in every respect. Their troubles and joys were so exactly alternated that the one was always in a position to condole or rejoice with the other. Did any mischance in business befall Gilliflower, would he go to his lawyer? Not he. He would say, "Send for Bardsley." Did Bardsley fall ill, would he send for the doctor? By no means. He sent for Gilliflower. And so they lived from youth to manhood, and from manhood to old age. I had the honour to be on pretty friendly terms with both of them, though much their junior, and I may say I grew old in their company. But I was never to Bardsley what Gilliflower was, nor to Gilliflower what Bardsley was. Far from it. I think I spoilt my claim to their full confidence by letting out early in our acquaintance that I knew something of Greek. I have wished from the bottom of my heart that Greece and Greek had never existed or been known, rather than I should have been deprived of the honour of sitting in the upper and inner chamber of two such hearts. I would have given all history to be Bardsley, all the glory of antiquity to be Gilliflower. Both men remained bachelors to the end of their days. People often wondered that they did not marry, they being both ardent, though respectful, admirers of the sex, and strongly attached to children. Many a time have I seen Bardsley sitting at his own door on a fine summer's evening playing with some curly-headed boy, or rosy-cheeked girl. He could repeat all the stories and rhymes that they delighted in; and Bardsley's knee was the cockhorse of many and many a journey to the famed cross of Banbury. Nor was that journey ever made in vain; for at the end of it there was always a halfpenny or a penny forthcoming from Bardsley's capacious pocket, to reward the youthful rider. And then Bardsley would say, "Now run away to Gilliflower's, my dear, and buy yourself some barley-sugar." And Gilliflower was known to the rising generation thereabouts to give the largest halfpenny-worth of barley-sugar of any grocer, far or near. And so fond were the children of the two old men—I am speaking of their latter days now,—that they called them by the names of "Uncle." Many a child of that neighbourhood grew up to man's estate, still calling them Uncle Bardsley and Uncle Gilliflower,—never doubting but that the two old men were as much their uncles in relationship as they were in kindness and affection. The reader may wonder, therefore, as the neighbours did, why two men so well adapted for the holy state of matrimony had never entered that state. I think I know why they did not. When Bardsley and Gilliflower first became acquainted (as the reader knows how) the former was beginning to have "serious thoughts" about a certain Jessy Ward, the niece of a well-to-do wax chandler in Toocum Street. He had seen Jessy at church on several occasions, and once he had walked home with her and her uncle. Old Ward asked him to tea, and he went and feasted upon Jessy's good looks and winning ways—having no appetite for the muffins—until, on coming away, he felt as if his heart was too big for his bosom. He could not sleep for several nights afterwards; and what seemed to keep him wakeful was the image of sweet Jessy Ward, and that strange bigness about the heart. But shortly after this Jessy went away to reside with an invalid aunt in the country, and did not come back for nearly a year. In the mean time Bardsley had got acquainted and become friendly with Gilliflower.

When Jessy returned he thought of going to call at old Ward's, and mentioned his intention to Gilliflower. What Gilliflower said I don't know; but at any rate Bardsley didn't go. I am sure that Gilliflower did not discourage him in any way; but my opinion is, that Bardsley conceived the idea that Gilliflower was not an advocate for matrimony, so he gave up all thoughts of Jessy Ward. Bardsley, however, was for once mistaken in his estimate of Gilliflower's views. I have reason to know that Gilliflower meditated matrimony at the same time that Bardsley did, but that he gave up the idea, fearful lest by taking a wife he should lose his friend. And so they remained bachelors for each other's sake to the end.

Alas that the end should ever come to such friendship as theirs. But it did come. The winter of life overtook them together as they wandered onward hand in hand. Its snows fell upon them equally, yet gently. No longer able to walk to their nightly resort, they now passed the evening at home, Bardsley going next door to Gilliflower, or Gilliflower going to Bardsley; or of a summer's evening they sat side by side at their doors, faithful to the last to the pipe and the flagon of ale. There, as they smoked and chatted as of old time, the children played around them, like flowerets twinkling about the roots of withered and decaying oaks. But an evening came when Gilliflower was no longer able to toddle out to meet his friend. Bardsley sat awaiting him, but he came not. Gilliflower's old housekeeper came to tell Bardsley that her master was very ill, and that she had helped him up to bed. The flagon of ale remained on the bench untasted, the pipes unused, the two chairs empty. Gilliflower had smoked his last pipe, and drunk his last flagon of ale. He grew feebler day by day, and at last his mind wandered. He raved about Bardsley: "Where is Bardsley? Oh, will some one send for Bardsley?" Bardsley was there by his side almost day and night; but his friend no longer knew him. I went in by Bardsley's request, to do what I could for his poor old friend, and I tried to make him understand that Bardsley was sitting by him, that it was Bardsley who was holding his hand.

"Go away, go away," he said; "you are not Bardsley. What use are you to me? it is Bardsley I want. Oh, if you will only send for him, I know he will come."

Then he raved about a bill that he fancied was coming due to-morrow, and for which he was not prepared. "I must go to Bardsley," he said, "Bardsley will help me out, I know he will. Give me my hat and stick."

"Hush, hush!" I cried; "Bardsley is here. Speak to him, Bardsley; let him hear your voice."

The old man called his friend by name. "Gilliflower, Gilliflower, it's me, Gilliflower, its Bardsley, your old friend."

"Eh? are you Bardsley?" he said at length, "Give me your hand. Ah! yes, it is Bardsley, my old friend, my good friend."

He sank for a short time into a slumber; but when he awoke he still called for Bardsley. He was with him again in thought at the Dragon.

"The pot is empty, Bardsley," he said. "Shall we have another; or shall we go home. I'll take a light, if you please—no, no, I won't trouble you, my pipe is out; we'll go home. Good night, Bardsley, good night; I shall see you again to-morrow."

As these words were uttered the hands of the two friends were clasped upon the bed. It was the clasp of death.

"I shall see you again to-morrow."

That to-morrow soon came. Poor Bardsley went on his earthly pilgrimage for a little while, seeking up and down for his friend Gilliflower. And one winter's night he made a long journey, and found him where there was no more parting.

YOU MUST DRINK!

There is no help for it—if you enter a public-house in England, you must drink. The whole system of licensed victualling has been carefully designed and elaborately built up, to compel people to drink and to prevent them from doing anything else. It is a mere mockery to call it victualling. Victuals have nothing to do with it, unless you are willing to dignify with that name, cold sausages, heart-cakes, and Abernethy biscuits. It was different in the old days, when innkeepers wrote over their doors, "Entertainment for Man and Beast." Entertainment for beast may still mean a cozy stall, a feed of corn and clean straw; but entertainment for man at all houses, not hotels, now means drink, wholly drink, and nothing but drink.

See how, in these days, the publican is constantly leading the human horse (and ass) to the gin-and-water, and compelling him to drink, whether he will or no. He plants his house at a corner with swing-doors on all sides, like so many man-traps; while he blazons his walls with golden legends, which tell of all that is fine, and pure, and double diamond, and old crusted, and over-proof, in drink. He sits like a syren in shirt-sleeves on this gilded rock, and regards all mankind as having one appetite—thirst; and one organ—throat. Enter this glittering temple of the one sense, and you leave all liberty of action behind. Suppose you are weary, and seat yourself on an empty barrel for a little while without immediately ordering refreshment. The publican looks at you reproachfully, as much as to say,

"You are a pretty fellow to come into my house and sit there without having anything to drink."

If you are slow to take the hint in looks, he will soon remind you of your duty in words,

"Now, sir, what can I serve you with?"

Order an Abernethy biscuit and a glass of water, and see how he will look at you! He keeps biscuits merely to *oblige* his customers, to accommodate the women chiefly; and heart-cakes to beguile the children, while father remains to have another glass. Biscuits, as a transaction, per se, he regards as an irregularity, only to be permitted on rare and special occasions, and only then under protest. As to water in its native purity, without the admixture of something strong—something that is worthy of exact measurement and can be charged for—that is altogether out of the question. Monstrous! He can scarcely bring himself to administer to the weary urchin, who comes in to beg a "drink of water" in the name of charity. He feels it beneath his dignity to dispense such poor stuff. Throughout all the branches of the trade there is a mad dog's horror of water, as such. If you go to a brewery and mention the word "water," you are immediately fined for the offence in gin; if you go to a distillery and mention the word "water," you are fined for the offence in beer. Say "liquor," and you are safe. The publican has no objection to aqua vitæ, or eau de vie; but call it the *water* of life, and he will be more shocked than if you used bad language.

It is curious how this antipathy to water, how this constant effort to make the public drink strong liquors and to debar them from every other entertainment, pervades the whole trade. Take the bar practice of the publican. He erects a great glittering temple of Bacchus, and by dividing it into uncomfortable pens, carefully unprovided with seats, compels votaries either to keep on sacrificing to the god or to go away.

At some halting-places in the City it is written up,

"Rest, but do not loiter." Here it is, "Do not loiter, but drink." The minute you have finished your glass it is whipped away; not unfrequently it is whipped away before you have finished it. You are made to feel that you have no right to remain in the place another moment, unless you renew your consumption. The publican's look says plainly, "Don't be a dog in a manger; if you won't drink yourself, stand aside and let others drink."

Observe how the British temple of Bacchus is adorned; what fine arts the High Priest employs to excite the devotional feelings of his flock. If you enter a similar temple in that benighted and slavish country, France, you will find many things designed to delight the eye and surround your indulgence with an air of elegance and comfort. There are chairs for you to sit upon, and little marble tables on which to rest your glass; for here you are not expected to empty liquor into yourself as from one vessel into another; and the walls are adorned with tasteful representations of fruit and flowers, and birds of gay plumage; with plaster casts, and statuettes, and other pleasing devices; while the counter glitters with vases full of real flowers, and elegant china dishes heaped with ripe and tempting fruits.

But what do we find in Britannia, which is the pride of the ocean, also the home of the brave and the free? The temple is glittering enough, and costly enough, truly; but you must stand up to your devotions, and get through them in a thorough business-like fashion. The walls are adorned with pictures, whose frames alone are worth all the French decorations put together—pictures by those great masters, Writer and Glazier, whose maxims written in letters of gold proclaim the virtues of Muggin's beer and Blotcher's gin, Burnmouth's brandy, and Liverburn's rum. Every panel contains a tablet of the law, which has but one commandment: "Thou shalt drink." Raise your eyes to the roof, and countless inscriptions on the beams lead you to the contemplation of that seventh heaven of delight to which you will be elevated if you obey the commandment and indulge in libations of Noseyman's port, or Blowout and Shandy's champagne of the finest brands. As for statuettes—behold Darby and Joan, and Daniel Lambert in ginger-beer bottle marble, with holes in their heads for spills, thus combining the useful with the beautiful. Fruit? Have you not the lemon sacred to the goddess of rum, and the divine gooseberry sublimated in champagne?

Let me say before I go any further, that this is not a teetotal article; and that I am not writing with the view of inducing any one to take the pledge. I set out with the admission, that strong drink is a very good thing in its way, and that to many thousands it is a necessary thing. Still, I cannot admit it to be the Alpha and Omega of all refreshment, and I protest against the system which makes all places, of so-called public entertainment, simply and purely drinking shops. The efforts of the publicans are every day more and more directed to this end.

Some few years ago, almost every public-house had its parlour and tap-room, the former devoted to the social foregatherings of neighbouring tradesmen, the latter provided with a fire and cooking utensils for the use of the labouring classes. The old-fashioned public-house parlour was the scene of right pleasant social meetings, after the labours of the day. Neighbours and cronies gathered together to discuss the affairs of the parish, or the politics of the nation, over a pipe, and a pint or two of ale, and it was the landlord's pleasure to occupy the chair, and play host, and treat his customers as guests and friends. It is true, that when the customers were rather too long over their pints, the waiter would come in and make a bungling pretence of stirring the fire or turning up the gas, by way of a hint; but it was a hint that no one was obliged to take. In most modern houses, however, the parlour and tap-room are done away with altogether, or converted into bars, where the customer comes like a bucket to a well, and fills himself and goes away again. There are very few places for friendly gatherings and social converse left. And those few that remain are made as uncomfortable as possible. All games, however innocent, are forbidden, not by the law, but by the publican, because they interfere with drinking. The harmless bagatelle-table has long been banished. Cards and even dominoes are interdicted on any pretence whatever. And here our wise and paternal legislature arms the publican with a pretence of authority by inserting in his license a clause forbidding him to suffer any unlawful games, or any gaming whatsoever, in his house, which the publican liberally interprets to mean that he is not to suffer any amusements, however innocent, which will divert the minds of his customers, and limit the consumption of drink. Fully sensible of the evils of gambling, I must, nevertheless, question the wisdom of the law, which is so careful to prevent a man losing small sums at a game of chance, while it takes pains to compel him to spend his money in drink. Gambling, bad as it is, is responsible for very few crimes in comparison with drink.

The effect of the public-house system as it

exists at present in all large towns, is to promote excessive drinking, for drinking sake, and to throw all the drinking, whether in excess or moderation, into the hands—or rather down the throats—of one class and one sex. The upper classes are independent of the public-house. They can afford to have all they require at home; and if they hunger or thirst when they are out of doors, they can afford to go to first-class hotels.

The rest of the population (for nearly all public purposes one class) is, in a great measure, dependent upon the public-house for out-door refreshment. But the public-house, being in all its departments a rough-and-ready stand-up constituted drink-shop, can be visited only by men. Few women not of a low class ever enter a London public-house; or, if they do, they sneak in with a sense of shame, conscious that it is a very unfit place for a decent woman to be seen in. Now, I hold that what is good for the goose is good for the gander; or rather in this case, I should say, what is good for the gander is good for the goose. Women require refreshment as well as men, and I believe it will not be denied that they are fond of a little social converse over a cup of tea, with, occasionally, a little drop of something in it. But, out of doors, they are wholly deprived of this; and in these days of railways and cheap excursions, women are almost as much out of doors as men.

The so-called house of public entertainment affords no fitting accommodation for respectable women; the rooms, where there are any, are not adapted for women, nor is the company. Men are so accustomed to congregate among themselves in drinking bars, and to use rough and indelicate language, that they cannot readily emancipate themselves from the *genius loci* even when a decent woman appears among them. They are apt to regard any woman who shows herself in such a place as no better than she should be. Thus the public-house system shuts out the great mass of women of the middle and lower classes from those necessaries, conveniencies, and pleasures which ladies of the upper class are enabled to enjoy, and do enjoy daily, at hotels. I cannot admit the pastrycook's to be any mitigation of this very hard case. Why cannot the people go to the pastrycook's for refreshment? Marie Antoinette said something of this kind when she was told that the people were starving for want of bread. "Why don't they eat sponge cakes?" she exclaimed. The truth is, that the pastrycook's is even less adapted to meet the wants of refreshment seekers than the public-house. Its eatables are chiefly puffs, and tarts, and sweetmeats; its drinkables, lemonade, ginger-beer, and cherry-brandy—matters calculated neither to appease the appetite nor to agree with the stomach. The prices are high, and the accommodation is limited. Men despise the pastrycook's. The new licensing act permits pastrycooks to sell wine; and in their windows, among the buns, and tarts, and sugarsticks, may now be seen little bottles of hock, and claret, and Moselle. This is a step in the right direction; but it is really of no advantage to any one while the pastrycook's shop is shunned by the men folks. Women don't like to sit and drink wine by themselves; they lack the courage to order it, though they are longing for a glass all the while.

How much better they manage these matters in France, where, as regards drink, there are no vested interests, no strictly guarded monopolies, and where the trade is, to a great extent, free and untrammelled! We boast in England of free trade; but, in this particular respect, we are far behind France. In that country, a public-house is a place combining elegance with comfort and convenience; its rooms are spacious, and handsomely appointed for the use of both sexes; refreshments of all kinds are served; and games and amusements are not only tolerated, but encouraged.

In a Parisian café you will find as many women as men—respectable women, too, who come with their husbands, and bring their children with them. There they sit in a family group round a marble table, sipping their coffee, or their wine, thinking it no shame to be seen by any of their neighbours, because there is nothing to be ashamed of. The café is not simply a drinking-shop. There is no necessity to drink anything stronger than coffee or *eau sucré;* and you may sit at your table as long as you please, read the paper, play at dominoes, or chat with your friends. All the amenities of private life are strictly observed. The men are gallant and polite; you never hear a word that could offend the most sensitive, and you never—or very rarely indeed—see any one tipsy. There is nothing about the place to suggest the drinking-shop, or to impress you with the obligation to drink. You feel that you are at liberty to take your ease and pleasure, and do as you like. So accustomed is the landlord to look upon his house as a place for the convenience and general entertainment of the public, that he will sometimes take more interest in a game of dominoes or piquet than in the vending of his goods. Madame will have to shriek to him to come and attend to his business. In Paris, even the lowest classes take their wine like gentlemen; in London, they swill their liquors like pigs. A London public-house is a trough.

It is strange that the philanthropists who are so zealous in the cause of temperance, and so anxious to promote sobriety among the people, have never sought to further their laudable object in the only way that is possible; namely, by attacking the licensing system. They can never hope to obtain a Maine Liquor Law; they can never hope to make the great body of the lower classes teetotallers. The public-house will exist in spite of them. This being granted, it simply remains for the friends of the people to take as much of the sting out of the public-house as possible, and to reduce its evils to the lowest.

This, I have no hesitation in saying, is only to be done by breaking up the existing monopoly, so elaborately built up, and so firmly maintained by the manufacturers and sellers of drink, and *throwing the trade open.* The tyranny of the British drink interest is something positively monstrous; and its power is complete. It dictates to the people what they shall drink, and what they shall not drink. It has been able almost entirely to defeat Mr Gladstone's measure for the reduction of the wine duties. The measure is law, but to all intents and purposes the law is a dead letter at public-houses. Good sound drinkable claret and Chablis can be sold in London for less money than in Paris, because the duty and the carriage together do not amount to so much as the octroi charged at the barriers of the latter city.

But the London publicans have combined to resist the introduction of these cheap and harmless wines; and hitherto with perfect success. Very few of them keep light French or German wines; and those who do charge four shillings a bottle for a wine which may be obtained from some of the new wine companies at twelve shillings a dozen. There are a few French and Italian restaurants in the neighbourhood of Leicester-square, where light French and German wines may be obtained at prices varying from one to three shillings a bottle. If I desire a substantial dinner off the joint, with the agreeable accompaniment of light wine, both cheap and good, I know of only one house, and that is in the Strand, close by Dane's Inn. There you may wash down the roast beef of old England with excellent Burgundy at two shillings a bottle, or you may be supplied with half a bottle for a shilling. Generally, however, at hotels and dining-rooms, four, five, six, and even seven shillings a bottle are still charged for ordinaire, dignified with the names of claret and Burgundy. The price is a prohibitive one, put on in the interests of British beer and spirits, and British port and sherry: which latter, in spite of the reduction of the duty, are still maintained at the old standard price of five shillings a bottle.

The publicans, while in this matter they tyrannize over the people, are themselves the slaves of those arch-tyrants, the brewers and distillers. They must not allow any liquors—not even good strong alcoholic port and sherry—to compete with native beer and gin. The only remedy for this state of things is the measure of which the teetotallers are most afraid—the throwing open of the trade. If those purblind philanthropists did not aim at a great Teetotal Utopia, they could not fail to be convinced by the simple logic of facts. Do away with an artificial and tyrannical monopoly, and you introduce a competition which must appeal to the suffrages and favour of the public. You make the public the masters instead of the slaves of those who serve them; and you make demand regulate supply instead of giving supply the power to control demand. A measure of this kind cannot fail to call into existence a new and improved class of refreshment-houses, and anything that tends to render these places fit resorts for the respectable classes of society of both sexes, must necessarily promote temperance and good manners. The laws of free trade are too well ascertained to leave any apprehension, even in the mind of a Chancellor of the Exchequer, of loss to the revenue in consequence of such a change. The same, if not a greater, quantity of drink will be consumed; but it will be shared more equally. It will no longer be dispensed by a monopoly of hands, nor swallowed by a monopoly of throats.

THE LAST OF THE TOLL-GATE.

"SHALL I go round the crescent, sir, and save the gate?"

It was thus that the unfeeling driver of a Hansom cab addressed me, through the trap in the roof of his vehicle, on the night of the 29th of June last.

"No, no," I said in tones of virtuous indignation. "Don't let us cheat a dying institution: go through, and let me pay my last twopence."

I am willing to confess that I had often been a consenting party to that détour round the crescent. Not that I ever saved anything by it, for the driver always looked for the twopence in addition to his fare, and always had it, taking it in the light of a reward of merit; but such is the rooted aversion of a free independent Briton, glorying in Magna Charta and popular representation, to anything in the shape of a tax for the support of those institutions in which he takes so much pride, that he will bestow his money upon the vilest of mankind rather than pay it into the hands of a paternal government, or any of its myrmidons. But on this occasion, the free and independent Briton was swayed by other feelings peculiar to his great nature. He was not going to hit an institution when it was down. So he went through the gate, and paid his twopence like a man.

The toll-keeper seemed to be also conscious of the touching and pitiful nature of the occasion. For the first time since I, the independent Briton, had, to my cost, known him, he spoke civilly, and, in giving me change out of sixpence, actually said, "Thank you, sir." Not to be outdone in this respect, I said, "You're very welcome, I'm sure, for it is the last twopence I shall pay you."

"Oh no, sir, I hope not," he replied. "There's all day to-morrow for you; we don't shut up for good, till twelve o'clock at night."

He seemed to say, "Don't despair, there is yet time and opportunity left to do a virtuous action." It was very kind of him. I was inclined to believe that to oblige me he would have been willing to continue the gate for a few days longer. I did not, however, desire that he should so far put himself out of the way on my account. I merely expressed my intention of paying a visit to the gate on the following day, delicately hinting at hospitality on my part. I was rejoiced to find that he would have no objection; that, in fact, he would be very happy to see me.

This was one of those happy hits which men make at random on the spur of the moment, and which are worth the best and most elaborate efforts of thought and deliberation. If the truth must be told, I had always regarded that toll-gate keeper with awe, nay, with some feeling of dread. Like many other persons in authority, he seemed to be encased in an armour of unapproachableness, hedged round by a divinity that repelled all familiar advances. With a strong disposition towards statistics and useful knowledge, I had for some time desired to make his acquaintance, and to learn from his own lips something of the philosophy and experience of toll-gate keeping.

I was curious to know whether the theory of a certain celebrated person with regard to the misanthropical nature of the pursuit was correct; or whether it was merely a malicious libel on the part of one who had been a victim to tolls. I was desirous to know if the keeper of a toll-gate regarded all mankind with the same aversion as all mankind regarded him; and perhaps I was curious to peep into the interior of that mysterious little round-house, and see a toll-keeper in the privacy of what might literally be called his domestic circle. I had long desired to fathom these things; but had never, with every elaboration of design, made the great advance towards them which I now achieved.

Until this happy moment, when a mutual sentiment brought us together on a friendly footing, I had signally failed in my endeavours to approach the keeper of that toll-gate. I had often strolled down to the gate with the intention of engaging him in conversation, but my courage invariably failed me. I was afraid that he might think me impertinent. Again and again I walked round the little house, in the hope that my timidity might miss its footing, and land me quite by accident in the confidence of the solemn functionary of whom all I knew was that his name was John Brown. In vain. I never succeeded in getting in his way, in running against him, in artfully contriving that he should run against me, or in any other way bringing myself under his notice. It would have been absurd to ask him the right time, for there was a big-faced clock in the front of the gate proclaiming the hour to all the passing world.

I thought at one time, in the pride of my knowledge of human nature, of approaching Mr Brown with a friendship's offering of a pot of beer extended in my hand; but I was warned against this course by the possibility (albeit I considered it a very bare one) of his being a teetotaller. I thought at another time, having observed that Mr Brown was addicted to the weed, of smoothing my way with a bundle of cigars: but was deterred by fear lest my motives might be misunderstood, and lest Mr Brown should suspect me to be a spy of the Trust. I may say that I beat about Mr Brown very much, learning many things from the perusal of the table of tolls concerning the charges for horses and asses, drawing and not drawing, and for waggons, vans, and carriages, the felloes of whose wheels were of certain dimensions, &c., but of Mr Brown himself, nothing.

When I walked down to the gate the following afternoon, I became sensible that a great sensation was prevailing in the neighbourhood. A great sensation had been prevailing in that neighbourhood for some considerable time; but now it was spreading out far and wide, like a rising flood, swamping the whole district in a deluge of excitement. There was a manifest tendency of the walking population "down the road," and a marked disposition on the part of the shopkeepers, to gather in knots on the pavement, as if they expected fireworks or a comet.

There was much discussion, too, which became more and more earnest as the gate was approached. I have reason to know that as a politician the High-street is thoroughly radical; that it has a great idea of free trade, reduced expenditure, and abolition of taxes; that it is great occasionally, at the Wilks and Liberty Hall in Lower Platform-street, on the rights of man, and the wrongs inflicted on society by a grasping hierarchy and a bloated aristocracy; that it is ready at any moment to vote for Blater and the right of meeting in the Parks, and that it hates all placemen, holders of sinecures, and the privileged classes generally. Yet, I found it to be the unanimous opinion of the High-street, more particularly towards its lower end, that the demolition of the toll-gate would be highly prejudicial to its interests, that it was a most unwarrantable and unconstitutional proceeding, and that it was directly inimical to the rights of man keeping shop in that vicinity. There was a decided disposition to connect the abolition of toll-gates in general, and of that toll-gate in particular, with the baleful influence of a grasping hierarchy and a bloated aristocracy; and I am sure that the connection would have been logically and conclusively established if the High-street had only seen how. to do it.

At one corner, the High-street, being interested in beer and the choicest spirits at dock-prices, including old vatted rum, was quite clear that in a mysterious manner not capable of lucid explanation, but indubitable nevertheless, the removal of the toll-gate would have much the same effect on beer and spirits as an advance in the price of hops, or an increase in the excise duty. A little higher up, the High-street, being interested in tobacco, as regards one window, and invisible perukes as regards the other, gloomily resigned itself to the conviction that when the gate was removed society at large would give up smoking, and cease to be bald. Next door but one, the High-street, being professionally engaged in making up gentlemen's own material, had also made up its mind that the gate and the habits of civilization would disappear together, and that mankind would, with the stroke of twelve that night, incontinently return to nudity and blue paint.

At a particular corner, on the pavement, the High-street being concerned in trotters, saw in the destruction of the gate a fatal blow to pork, tending to the ultimate extinction of that useful though not ornamental animal, the pig; at the same time opening up a broad and clear road leading to the workhouse. In fact, the High-street, though thoroughly radical when other persons are concerned, was on this occasion, when the party concerned was the High-street itself, eminently conservative.

On the other hand, the drivers and conductors of cabs and omnibuses, whose interests lay in a different direction, and whose views had no doubt been enlarged by a daily survey of mankind from 'Igate to the Habbey, contemplated the dissolution of the gate with undisguised satisfaction, while the juvenile population, at all times strongly iconoclastic, was preparing to celebrate the occasion in a becoming manner, and to seize the earliest moment, when the protection of the law should be withdrawn, to break the toll-gate's windows.

Through this terrible war of mental elements I made my way to the doomed gate, and accosting Mr Brown, hoped I saw him well, or at least as well as could be expected under the melancholy circumstances. How often it happens in life that the man whom, when you did not know him, you regarded as haughty and unapproachable, proves, when you do come to know him, to be the most affable fellow imaginable! I had not been two minutes in Mr Brown's company, before I perceived that in walking round him and beating about him I had entirely mistaken Mr Brown's nature and wasted my own time. I might have approached him with a peace-offering of a pot of beer, and been received with joy; I might have paved the way with a bundle of cigars, and found it the direct road to his affections. I imagined him to be a great frozen block of reserve, but I knew now that I might have melted him throughout with three-pen'orth warm. I conceived him to be a pillar of darkness; I discovered that I might have lighted him up with a pickwick.

Would Mr Brown take anything? Mr Brown's ready apprehension of the significance of this masonic form of interrogatory made me almost painfully sensible of the absurdity of having suspected him of teetotalism. Mr Brown would take *anything*, but, for choice, old ale. The way in which one of Mr Brown's boys, on receiving a shilling, annihilated time and space, and disappeared through a double swing door leading to the region of old vatted rum, was suggestive of lightning. Did Mr Brown smoke? Mr Brown, casting his eye towards the tall red chimney that erected itself from the flat roof of the toll-gate like an inflamed mark of admiration, said that he *could*: evidently implying that, as regards smoking, a flue with a short draught was a fool to him. For choice, Mr Brown took returns —and I had hesitated to approach him with regalias!

Was Mr Brown sorry that the gate was about to be done away with? This timidly and gingerly, lest Mr Brown might resent any interference with his private affairs. But Mr Brown had no reserve. He put himself at once on the footing of a sworn witness on a highway committee.

"Sorry! Lor' bless you, sir, I shall be jolly glad when twelve o'clock comes, and it's all over. You wouldn't believe the life the 'busmen and the cabbies have been a leading me for a week past; ah, for a month a'most. To-day it has been dreadful. And you may be as good at chaff as you like, but you can't have an answer ready for every one. Me and my boys have been making up things to say all the morning, and we've given it to a few of them pretty hot, though, of course, some of them had the best of us. There's a surly old fellow as generally goes round the crescent and evades the gate when he can, but the other day he was obliged to come through.

"'Ah!' he says, 'there will be no gates after Friday.'

"'Oh yes there will,' I says; 'they're going to leave one on your account.'

"'Which gate is that?' he says.

"'Why, Newgate!' I says.

"You should have seen how he whipped into his horse and made off double quick. Then there's a saucy, cheeky sort of a chap as drives a Hansom says to me:

"'Hullo, John!" he says, 'what are you going to do when the gate's down? Start a baked tatur can, or go into the catch-'em-alive-oh line?'

"'No, neither,' I says, 'but I don't mind telling you what I intend to be up to. I'm going to do something to be put into the house of correction, and when I come out with a ticket-of-leave I'll be fully qualified to drive a cab.'"

While Mr Brown was thus discoursing in the most communicative manner, he was constantly under the necessity of breaking off short to run and take the tolls; or, if it were not a vehicle of sufficient importance for his own notice, to shout to his two boys to take the tolls for him. And the two boys were always scurrying out into the roads and scurrying back again to drop coppers into the capacious pockets of Mr Brown's white apron.

"There's some folks think, sir, that toll-keeping is an easy, idle kind of life. They only see me for a minute as they go by, and that's all they know about it. If they was to stand here fourteen hours a day, as I do, they'd know different. You're never at rest a minute; there's always something a-going through. It's no use to sit down; you can't sit for two minutes together; and getting up and down like that is very trying to the legs. I know what toll-keeping is, sir. I've been in it all my life. I was born in a toll-gate down at Pangbourne—it wasn't like this, you know, it had rooms and all kind of convenience—and that, perhaps, *was* easy; but here in London it's almost as bad as the treadmill; that is, I should say it was, sir; of course I don't know for certain. It's not what it was, toll-keeping. Everything's redooced so, now-a-days. We're obliged to make a reduction for taking a quantity. Why, there's forty 'busses goes through this gate, each, on a average, fourteen times every day, and we take the lot for ten pound a week. It would be more than ten times that, if we were to make them pay every time. But if we had done that, there wouldn't have been half the 'busses on this road. When a company thinks of starting, they come to us and say, 'What will you take us for?' And we say, so much; and if it's what they can afford, they come on the road, and if it's more than they can afford, they don't. But we're always liberal, sir. We let the cabs pass free when they're empty; that ain't a right, sir; it's a privilege which we allow them. And what's the return they make for that privilege? Why, when they've got a fare they go round the crescent, and then when they're empty they come back through the gate. That's what a cabman calls gratitude. I've known them flash little bits of newspaper cut up to look like tickets, to the boys when they've been larking and not taking much notice. I've been done that way myself, once or twice; I've caught a few out, though. I remember my old master, Mr Levy, the contractor, bowling a cab-driver out in fine style. The man, after driving him more than a hundred yards on the Trust, took him sharp up the side of the crescent, and so evaded the toll. When he set Mr Levy down at his house, and he'd paid his right fare, he says, 'Ain't you going to give me the twopence for evading the gate?' 'No,' Mr Levy says, 'I won't do that, but as I'm the contractor for the tolls, I'll give you a summons as early as I can to-morrow morning.' And he did too; but he was a good sort, and wouldn't have taken no notice if the man hadn't been cheeky. I used to collect the post-duty under Mr Levy; that was in the old coaching times, before railways. My station was down near King's Cross, and I used to take the tickets as the post-chaises went by, some of them bound for Gretna-green; for somehow or other, sir, lovers were fond of running away to be married when it was a hard job to do it; but now, when there's railways and it's easy, they don't seem to care about it. Human nature, I suppose, sir? But taking post-duty was better than toll-keeping. I used to get a penny on every ticket, and I've often earned as much as eight pound a week. But the post-duty was done away with, and now the tolls is to be done away with. This gate has had a good many shoves at one time or another. It was up at St Giles's once; but they shoved it on gradually to here, and now it's to be shoved right out into the country somewhere. No; I don't think I shall go with it; but I ain't afraid. I've always found that when one gate shuts another opens. A gent said to me to-day, 'Why Mr Brown,' he says, 'with your figure and your aprons, you would be a credit to Doctors' Commons.' I'll drop into something, I dare say. I've been taking stock of the traffic on this road for the railway bill, and perhaps I'll get a job to take tickets for Puffing Billy. The 'busses and the cabs are all rejoicing because the tolls is to be done away with; but I tell them it will be all the worse for them in the end. Puffing Billy will come and knock them all off the road. No; I don't pay a rent for the toll. The contractor trusts me to do the best I can for him."

After an interval for refreshment and the quiet digestion of all this toll lore, I revisited the gate at about eleven o'clock. The excitement was intense now. The little house was surrounded by a crowd of two or three hundred persons, male and female, the youthful portion showing a strong disposition to dance. Many of Mr Brown's personal friends had arrived, and were inside the toll-house, drinking Mr Brown's health. Beer was coming over from the public-house—in pots at first, in cans presently, eventually, as the hour of doom approached, in pails. Presenting myself at the door of the house, I was refused admission, but, on being recognized by Mr Brown, was admitted—to the great envy of the unprivileged classes outside, who seemed to regard me somewhat in the light of one who had the entrée at court. Inside, Mr Brown's friends were drinking out of the pots, out of the cans, out of the pails. Beer, beer everywhere, not only to drink but to stand in, sit in, swim in, if any one had been so inclined. Beer, too, was going on outside. The hilarity was becoming fast and furious. Mr Brown was delighted. He put himself in the position of a host giving an al fresco nocturnal fête. He was glad to see everybody; anxious to make everybody happy. Music was suggested. Mr Brown procured a boy with a tin whistle. The tin whistle being voted weak and inadequate to the occasion, Mr Brown sent to some neighbouring depôt of music and secured the services of a band, consisting of a cornet-à-piston, a trombone, and a drum. Beer having been administered to the band, it was hoisted up on to the roof of the gate-house, from which elevated position it played many favourite selections, while the mob below danced a sort of Carmagnole round the toll-house.

A stranger coming up at that moment would have found it difficult to say, in view of the buckets of beer which still continued to be carried across, whether the occasion were a fire; or, in view of the wild revolutionary dance, whether the toll-house were a sort of Bastille, and the people were taking it by assault! Every vehicle that arrived was immediately surrounded by the mob, who seemed to derive some sort of savage satisfaction from seeing the last tolls paid. Wild shouts hailed the surrender of every two-pence, as if (taking the revolutionary view of the matter), the coins were the heads of tyrants falling under the stroke of the guillotine. Heavily laden omnibuses dashed through the crowd in triumph, the drivers flourishing their whips, the occupants of the knife-board standing up and waving hats and handkerchiefs, while the conductors, with that politeness which distinguishes them, took sights at Mr Brown, and shouted "Ya-ah!" at him as if he had been a wild beast having his teeth filed and his claws cut.

Time advances. Beer is hoisted up to the band in a bucket, and in a moment of impatient waiting for music, when all eyes are directed to the elevated orchestra, the trombone is seen upon all fours drinking like a horse. Inside the house Mr Brown's friends, too numerous for the limited accommodation, are beginning to drop and drag themselves among the beer, suggesting bluebottles on a sloppy public-house counter. Considering that before the close of the proceedings beer actually found its way through the roof, it was a mercy some of them were not drowned.

"A quarter to twelve. Hurrah! Ten minutes to twelve. Hurrah!" A cab comes up with an unprotected female in it. The cab is immediately surrounded by the mob, and the unprotected female turns pale and shrieks. She is assured that it is not her life that is wanted, but only her twopence. A hundred hands are held out for the money, and though it is taken by strangers, it is immediately handed over to Mr Brown. "Five minutes to twelve! Only five minutes more, Brown; suppose we burn the gate, and finish up with a bonfire!" Mr Brown is so good-humoured, and so thoroughly enjoying his "breaking-up," that I really believe he would have made no objection to this proposition if it could have been carried into execution without immolating his friends. I doubt, however, if the toll-house in its then saturated state would have burned readily.

"One minute to twelve! Hurrah! hurrah!! hurrah!!!" A tremendous shout this time; the band, with a dim apprehension of the nature of the occasion, fatuously playing the Death of Nelson. A cab appears with another unprotected female, who, amid frantic acclamations, pays the last toll. "Twelve!" The protection and countenance of the law being withdrawn from the toll-house, crash goes a shower of Macadam through its windows. Happily Mr Brown's friends are all prostrate, and the consequences are not tragic. Another shout, to which Mr Brown responds by taking off and waving his white apron. And all is over.

Passing along a day or two after, I found nothing to mark the spot where the gate had stood but a little blue patch of Macadam, under which one might have supposed the toll-house to be buried. I hear, however, that the gate is not dead yet; that it has had another shove; and that, while being dragged bodily up the Euston-road by two horses, for whose strength and spirits it was a great deal too much, it was given into custody by a member of the Society for the Prevention of Cruelty to Animals.

THE AUTHOR OF "BLUEBLAZES."

WHEN the remarkable romance, entitled "Blueblazes," was first published, I, in common with the whole of the reading world, was seized with an intense desire to know the Author. I need not remind any one that "Blueblazes" was an anonymous work, for that circumstance, having given as much impetus to its fame as anything, is intimately connected with its popularity. It will be fresh in the recollection of all who take a close interest in literary matters, that the critics of the period displayed much logical and inferential acumen in their endeavours to prove to a demonstration what already celebrated author had, as regarded "Blueblazes," indulged in the freak of literary masquerading. How the great Abecedarian George was softly impeached of "Blueblazes," though from the absence from the work of two horsemen of opposite mien and aspect, it must be confessed, on the most slender and inconclusive evidence. How, even the famous Sir Edward himself, "England's first and most distinguished author," did not escape the passing suspicion of having done a good thing, and scorned to tell it: how, at length, when collations and comparisons had been exhausted, the literary world settled down into a sort of passive belief that the authorship of "Blueblazes" belonged, not to any man who had already distinguished himself, but to some new and unknown genius, who, either from motives of modesty, or perhaps vanity, shrank from proclaiming himself to the world.

It was hoped by those who took a deep interest in "Blueblazes," that the encouragement bestowed by the public upon the unknown author might tempt him, in subsequent works, to declare himself. But this hope was destined to be disappointed. His second well-known work, "Pompey's Pillar," was simply announced as "by the Author of 'Blueblazes.'" The secret was still kept, and each succeeding work from the same pen (though, by the general voice, all inferior to the original "Blueblazes") only served to keep alive and intensify the curiosity of the public. In time, the authorship of "Blueblazes" became a companion mystery to the authorship of "Junius."

As a young man, following the pursuit of letters, I naturally took a deep interest in this much-vexed question. The perusal of "Blueblazes" had inspired me with boundless admiration. I did, with regard to that book, what I never did before, or have done since, with regard to any book at the price of one pound eleven and sixpence—I bought it. I read it again and again. I lent it to my friends. I talked about it everywhere. I constructed theories as to the authorship, and swore by them one after the other—which only served to involve me in still greater perplexity and doubt; for examining the work of one writer with that of another, with the purpose of tracing points of resemblance, is like reading Buchan's "Domestic Medicine"—in the latter case you fancy you have every disease you read of; and in the former you fancy you discover traces of identity in every page. There was not an author of heroic romance upon whom I had not affiliated "Blueblazes."

At last I came round to the prevailing theory, that the author was a new man; and as this conclusion, while the said new man persisted in maintaining the mystery respecting himself, precluded all further attempts to solve the problem by the force of logic or reason, I was fain to subside and settle down into an equable contemplation of a subject, which had baffled all my skill. So, like the rest of the world, I slackened my pace, and as regarded "Blueblazes," went along steadily. At any moment, however, I should have been ready to start off afresh, if any clue had been discovered leading to the solution of the great mystery; but for some time nothing occurred to revive the topic. At length, however, something did occur. I had been dining with a few friends at a well-known tavern, and we were sitting discussing the punch, which appears to be an inevitable sequitur of all dinners there, when a friend, who sat next to me, whispered in my ear,—

"Do you see that queer-looking old gentleman in the brown wig, at the other table?"

Yes, I saw him; and he was, as my friend observed, a decidedly queer-looking old gentleman. I saw at a glance a large pale face, ornamented with a large blossoming nose, two small round eyes unadorned by any eye-lash whatever, a slit of a mouth extending almost from one very large flap of an ear to another very large flap of an ear.

I saw a brown wig above this picture, and a wispy white choker below it.

"Yes, I see him," I said.

"Well," said my friend, "that is the author of 'Blueblazes.'"

"You should never speak, or laugh, when your mouth is full," is a valuable piece of advice, which I duly received on making my first appearance in the company of grown-up people "at table."

And it is one which I had always striven to follow; but this startling communication, falling upon my ear at a moment when I was holding suspended in my mouth a gulp of punch, took my manners unawares, and completely upset them! The punch went all sorts of wrong ways, and ended its evolutions by nearly choking me. Recovering myself, I appealed to the company,

"What do you think C—— says? I can scarcely tell you for laughing; it is something so absurd, so positively ridiculous—he says that that ridiculous-looking old fogy at the other table is the author of 'Blueblazes!'"

I fully expected that my friends would join in the derisive laughter with which the notion affected me; but instead of that they one and all maintained a most serious air, and said in chorus—

"Well, he *is* the author of 'Blueblazes.'"

"Are you serious," I asked—"really serious?"

"My dear fellow," said C——, in a confidential tone, and with the utmost gravity, "I was not joking; there is no doubt about it whatever."

One of our company here went across to where the great author sat, and shaking him cordially by the hand, invited him to take a seat at our table. He was now among us, and at length there was only the distance of a table between me and that great man, whose genius had inspired me with such high admiration, and whom I had been so anxious to know and become acquainted with. After feasting my hungry eyes upon the lineaments of the great person, and discovering bumps and developments all over him, unmistakeably proclaiming him a man of no ordinary stamp, I whispered to C—— that I should like to be introduced to him. C—— immediately complied, and said,—"Mr Bagshaw, allow me to introduce our friend here."

His name, then, was Bagshaw! Mr Bagshaw smiled and bowed, and was good enough to offer me his hand. I need not say that I shook it with pride, and said, as best I could, in the nervous flutter into which I had been thrown, how highly I esteemed the honour of making the acquaintance of one so greatly distinguished as the Author of "Blueblazes."

I then relapsed into silence, and gave way to reflections with respect to the off-hand manner in which genius is too frequently treated by nature and fate. "Here," I exclaimed, inwardly, "is a genius of the highest order, who is personally as ugly as Punch, and whose name is Bagshaw! Unkind Nature! Cruel Fate!"

The Author of "Blueblazes" became my almost intimate friend. He was not like some geniuses that we all wot of, who forget the persons they have once known, and who make it a rule never to acknowledge any one who is not either rich, or as high up as themselves. Meeting him in the street about a week after the red-letter day on which I had made his acquaintance, I ventured to nod to him. Did he look as if he did not know me, and pass by on the other side of the way? Not he. He not only returned my nod, but stopped and shook me by the hand quite kindly. Nor was he in any hurry to get away from me, but remained and chatted until the usual street-corner topics were exhausted, when he shook hands again in parting. I was enraptured by his condescension. I could, indeed, call the Author of "Blueblazes," "my friend." And I did not neglect to minister to my own glory by doing so whenever opportunity offered. "The Author of 'Blueblazes,'" I would say, "oh, I know him very well—he is my most intimate friend—his name is Bagshaw—I had the honour of taking luncheon with him yesterday."

Yes; after knowing Mr Bagshaw for about a week, I did very frequently have the honour of taking luncheon with him. He was not too proud to take luncheon *with me*, and would adjourn, at my solicitation, to a chop, and even a sausage. I offered port at first, as more suitable to the palate of high genius; but I soon found that half-and-half was not despised, and that gin and water and a pipe were apparently held in as high esteem as claret and a cigar. At length, the Author of "Blueblazes" would take my arm, and go for a stroll. These were proud moments! Meeting my acquaintances, I could stop, shake hands with them, and whisper in their ears,—"This gentleman is the author of 'Blueblazes.'" Then, leaving them abruptly, I would look behind me, and see them gazing after the great man on my arm, with looks of awe and admiration.

The condescension of the Author of "Blueblazes" was such as I could never have imagined in one so celebrated and exalted. He would not only take a "snack" with me, but would allow me to pay the bill; and he has even gone so far as to take a glass of ale with me at a tavern bar. But the cup of my pride fairly ran over, when the great creature accepted my invitation to dinner, at home. He arrived punctually, and greatly delighted me by doing the most ample justice to everything I had provided for him.

Mr Bagshaw was a singularly modest man for an author. Until this occasion, I had never heard him make any direct reference to his own great work. In the course of a conversation on authors over the second bottle of claret, he suddenly broke out with,—"The Author of 'Blueblazes' has observed," &c. "That is to say," I interposed, "you yourself have observed, Mr Bagshaw." The Author of "Blueblazes" smiling a modest, self-convicted smile, said, "You are very good," and sipped his wine.

"In many respects, Mr Bagshaw," I presently observed, "your second great work, 'Pompey's Pillar,' is superior in my opinion to 'Blueblazes.' It has, for example, a higher purpose."

"I am glad," said Mr Bagshaw, "you think so. The observation you have made is very correct, though the critics have not generally recognized the truth of it. The purpose of 'Pompey's Pillar' is decidedly higher."

In process of time I became quite used to the Author of "Blueblazes." I met him frequently, was privileged to call him Bagshaw, and at length attained, in my own mind, a high literary eminence from his companionship. It was no longer an honour to me to make the acquaintance of literary celebrities; for was I not the intimate friend of the Author of "Blueblazes"?

The Author of "Blueblazes" had been my friend and companion for more than a year, when one day I read in the Art Gossip of a newspaper that the walls of a certain exhibition of pictures were "graced by a portrait of the Author of

'Blueblazes.'" The writer added that the portrait was that of a lady. My first impulse was to write to the Editor of the paper, and point out the lamentable mistake; but on second thoughts I determined to visit the exhibition, and ascertain for myself how such an absurd blunder could have been committed. Accordingly, I provided myself with a catalogue, and went straight to the gallery. In the catalogue I found—"No. 90 Portrait of the Author of 'Blueblazes.'" I looked about for the well-known lineaments of my friend, but could nowhere observe them. At length I came upon "No. 90." What did I see? Not the fine classic head, the piercing eye, and the other highly intellectual features of my friend Bagshaw, but the portrait of a charming young lady in curls. What did this mean? Some mistake had occurred—the numbers had been misplaced—the catalogue was in error. Failing to obtain any satisfactory information from the attendants, and burning with indignation at the injustice which had been done to my friend, I rushed off to my club, to communicate the discovery to my literary friends. Luckily I found my friend C—— there. I told him, with great excitement of manner, the whole story; but I saw by the smile on his countenance that he knew it already.

"But what does it mean?" I asked.

"Mean! my dear fellow," said C—— with a shrug, "It means this; that our friend Bagshaw is blown upon. He is not the author of 'Blueblazes.' So far as I can understand, he was the agent who transacted the business with the publisher. The publisher thought he was the author, and so we came to think so too. Bagshaw favoured the notion, and has traded upon this false reputation to some extent. He has got into good society, has been treated, and flattered, and pointed at, and made a lion of. This affair has stripped him of his lion's skin; and he now returns to the original ass—which, by the by, I always thought, in my own private mind, was his true character."

I have only to add, that Bagshaw suddenly disappeared, and from that day to this has never been seen in the old haunts. He is still remembered, however, by those who, like myself, were deluded out of reverence and rum and water by his assumption to be the AUTHOR of "BLUEBLAZES."

END OF VOL. I.

CPSIA information can be obtained
at www.ICGtesting.com
Printed in the USA
LVHW040025180422
716440LV00005B/416

9 783752 593709